D0553669

Tony DiTerlizzi *and* Holly Black

Simon and Schuster Books for Young Readers
New York London Toronto Sydney

SIMON & SCHUSTER BOOKS FOR YOUNG READERS
An imprint of Simon & Schuster Children's Publishing Division
1230 Avenue of the Americas, New York, New York 10020

Book design by Tony DiTerlizzi and Dan Potash
Manufactured in the United States of America
10 9 8 7 6 5 4 3 2 1
CIP data for this book is available from the Library of Congress.
ISBN-13: 978-1-4169-5821-5
ISBN-10: 1-4169-5821-5

Jared looked around the room.

Tony DiTerlizzi *and* Holly Black

Simon and Schuster Books for Young Readers
New York London Toronto Sydney Singapore

SIMON & SCHUSTER BOOKS FOR YOUNG READERS
An imprint of Simon & Schuster Children's Publishing Division
1230 Avenue of the Americas, New York, New York 10020

 • Book design by Tony DiTerlizzi and Dan Potash • Manufactured in the United States of America

20

Library of Congress Cataloging-in-Publication Data
Black, Holly.
The field guide / Holly Black and Tony DiTerlizzi.
p. cm.— (The Spiderwick chronicles ; 1)
Sequel: The seeing stone.
Summary: When the Grace children go to stay at their great-aunt Lucinda's worn Victorian house, they discover a field guide to fairies and other creatures and begin to have some unusual experiences.
ISBN 0-689-85936-8
[1. Fairies—Fiction. 2. Brothers and sisters—Fiction.]
I. DiTerlizzi, Tony. II. Title.
PZ7.B52878 War 2003
[Fic]—dc21
2002013524

For my grandmother, Melvina,
who said I should write a book just like this one
and to whom I replied that I never would
—H. B.

For Arthur Rackham,
may you continue to inspire others
as you have me
—T. D.

Table of
Contents

List of Full-Page
Illustrations

Dear Reader,

Over the years that Tony and I have been friends, we've shared the same childhood fascination with faeries. We did not realize the importance of that bond or how it might be tested.

One day Tony and I—along with several other authors—were doing a signing at a large bookstore. When the signing was over, we lingered, helping to stack books and chatting, until a clerk approached us. He said that there had been a letter left for us. When I inquired which one of us, we were surprised by his answer.

"Both of you," he said.

The letter was exactly as reproduced on the following page. Tony spent a long time just staring at the photocopy that came with it. Then, in a hushed voice, he wondered aloud about the remainder of the manuscript. We hurriedly wrote a note, tucked it back into the envelope, and asked the clerk to deliver it to the Grace children.

Not long after, a package arrived on my doorstep, bound in red ribbon. A few days after that, three children rang the bell and told me this story.

What has happened since is hard to describe. Tony and I have been plunged into a world we never quite believed in. We now see that faeries are far more than childhood stories. There is an invisible world around us and we hope that you, dear reader, will open your eyes to it.

HOLLY BLACK

Dear Mrs. Black and Mr. DiTerlizzi:

I know that a lot of people don't believe in faeries, but I do and I think that you do too. After I read your books, I told my brothers about you and we decided to write. We know about real faeries. In fact, we know a lot about them.

The page attached* to this one is a photocopy from an old book we found in our attic. It isn't a great copy because we had some trouble with the copier. The book tells people how to identify faeries and how to protect themselves. Can you please give this book to your publisher? If you can, please put a letter in this envelope and give it back to the store. We will find a way to send the book. The normal mail is too dangerous.

We just want people to know about this. The stuff that has happened to us could happen to anyone.

Sincerely,

Mallory, Jared, and Simon Grace

*Not included.

THE JUNKYARD
THE
ROUNTREE STREET
THE BRIDGE
THE SPIDERWICK ESTATE
DULAC DRIVE
THE GROVE

To Town
The Old Quarry
J. Waterhouse Middle School
Riccenbach Way
Robinson Creek
N
Map of the
Spiderwick Estate
and
Surrounding Areas

THE
SPIDERWICK
CHRONICLES

It was more like a dozen shacks.

Chapter One

IN WHICH the Grace Children Get Acquainted with Their New Home

If someone had asked Jared Grace what jobs his brother and sister would have when they grew up, he would have had no trouble replying. He would have said that his brother, Simon, would be either a veterinarian or a lion tamer. He would have said that his sister, Mallory, would either be an Olympic fencer or in jail for stabbing someone with a sword. But he couldn't say what job he would grow up to have. Not that anyone asked him. Not that anyone asked his opinion on anything at all.

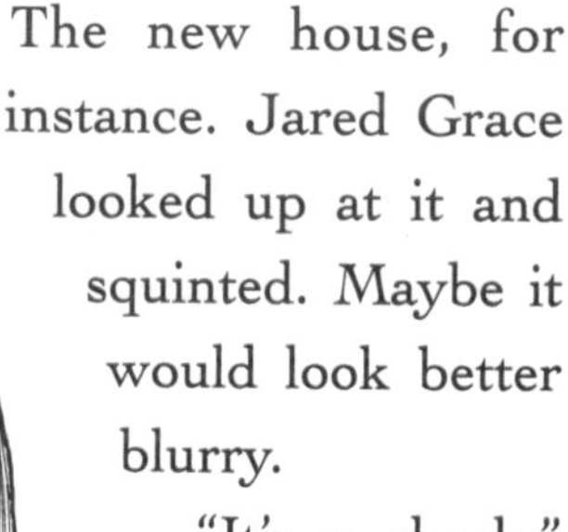

The new house, for instance. Jared Grace looked up at it and squinted. Maybe it would look better blurry.

"It's a shack," Mallory said, getting out of the station wagon.

It wasn't really, though. It was more like a dozen shacks had been piled on top of one another. There were several chimneys, and the whole thing was topped off by a strip of iron fence sitting on the roof like a particularly garish hat.

"It's not so bad," their mother said, with a smile

that looked only slightly forced. "It's Victorian."

Simon, Jared's identical twin, didn't look upset. He was probably thinking of all the animals he could have now. Actually, considering what he'd packed into their tiny bedroom in New York, Jared figured it would take a lot of rabbits and hedgehogs and whatever else was out here to satisfy Simon.

SIMON GRACE

"Come on, Jared," Simon called. Jared realized that they had all crossed to the front steps and he was alone on the lawn, staring at the house.

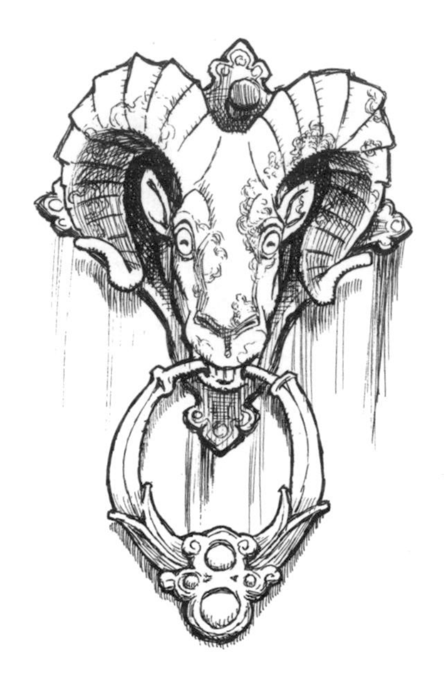

The doors were a faded gray, worn with age. The only traces of paint were an indeterminate cream, stuck deep in crevices and around the hinges. A rusted ram's-head door knocker hung from a single, heavy nail at its center.

Their mother fit a jagged key into the lock, turned it, and shoved hard with her shoulder.

The door opened into a dim hallway. The only window was halfway up the stairs, and its stained glass panes gave the walls an eerie, reddish glow.

"It's just like I remember," she said, smiling.

"Only crappier," said Mallory.

Their mother sighed but didn't otherwise respond.

The hallway led into a dining room. A long table with faded water spots was the only piece of furniture. The plaster ceiling was cracked in places and a chandelier hung from frayed wires.

"Why don't you three start bringing things in from the car?" their mother said.

"Into here?" Jared asked.

"Yes, into here." Their mother put down her suitcase on the table, ignoring the eruption of dust. "If your great-aunt Lucinda hadn't let us stay, I don't know where we would have gone. We should be grateful."

None of them said anything. Try as he might, Jared didn't feel anything close to grateful. Ever since their dad moved out, everything had gone bad. He'd messed up at school, and the fading bruise over his left eye wouldn't let him forget it. But this place—this place was the worst yet.

"Jared," his mother said as he turned to follow Simon out to unload the car.

"What?"

His mother waited until the other two were down the hall before she spoke. "This is a chance to start over . . . for all of us. Okay?"

Jared nodded grudgingly. He didn't need her to say the rest of it—that the only reason he hadn't gotten kicked out of school was because they were moving anyway. Another reason he was supposed to be grateful. Only he wasn't.

Outside, Mallory had stacked two suitcases on top of a steamer trunk. "I heard she's starving herself to death."

"Aunt Lucinda? She's just old," said Simon. "Old and crazy."

But Mallory shook her head. "I heard Mom on the phone. She was telling Uncle Terrence that Aunt Lucy thinks little men bring her food."

"What do you expect? She's in a nuthouse," Jared said.

Mallory went on like she hadn't heard him. "She told the doctors the food she got was better than anything they'd ever taste."

"You're making that up." Simon crawled into the backseat and opened one of the suitcases.

Mallory shrugged. "If she dies, this place is going to get inherited by someone, and we're going to have to move again."

"Maybe we can go back to the city," Jared said.

"Fat chance," said Simon. He took out a wad of tube socks. "Oh, no! Jeffrey and Lemondrop chewed their way loose!"

"Mom told you not to bring the mice," Mallory said. "She said you could have *normal* animals now."

"If I let them go, they'd get stuck in a glue trap or something," said Simon, turning a sock inside out, one finger sticking out a hole. "Besides, you brought all your fencing junk!"

"It's not junk," Mallory growled. "And it's not *alive.*"

"Shut up!" Jared took a step toward his sister.

"Just because you've got one black eye

doesn't mean I can't give you another one." Mallory flipped her ponytail as she turned toward him. She shoved a heavy suitcase into his hands. "Go ahead and carry that if you're so tough."

Even though Jared knew he might be bigger and stronger than her someday—when she wasn't thirteen and he wasn't nine—it was hard to picture.

Jared managed to lug the suitcase inside the door before he dropped it. He figured he could drag it the rest of the way if he had to and no one would be the wiser. Alone in the hallway of the house, however, Jared no longer remembered how to get to the dining room. Two different hallways split off this one, winding deep into the middle of the house.

"Mom?" Although he'd meant to call out loudly, his voice sounded very soft, even to himself.

"Mom?"

No answer. He took a tentative step and then another, until the creak of a board under his feet stopped him.

Just as he paused, something *inside* the wall rustled. He could hear it scrabbling upward, until the sound disappeared past the ceiling. His heart beat hard against his chest.

It's probably just a squirrel, he told himself. After all, the house looked like it was falling apart. Anything could be living inside; they'd be lucky if there wasn't a bear in the basement and birds in all the heating ducts. That was, if the place even *had* heat.

"Mom?" he said again, even more faintly.

Then the door behind him opened and Simon came in, carrying mason jars with two bug-eyed gray mice in them. Mallory was right behind him, scowling.

"I heard something," Jared said. "In the wall."

"What?" Simon asked.

"I don't know. . . ." Jared didn't want to admit that for a moment he'd thought it was a ghost. "Probably a squirrel."

Simon looked at the wall with interest. Brocaded gold wallpaper hung limply, peeling and pocking in places. "You think so? In the house? I always wanted a squirrel."

No one seemed to think that something in the walls was anything to worry about, so Jared didn't say anything more about it. But as he carried the suitcase to the dining room, Jared couldn't help thinking about their tiny apartment in New York and their family before the divorce. He wished this was some kind of gimmicky vacation and not real life.

The creak startled him into jerking upright.

Chapter Two

IN WHICH Two Walls Are Explored by Vastly Different Methods

The leaks in the roof had made all but three of the upstairs bedroom floors dangerously rotted. Their mother got one, Mallory got another, and Jared and Simon were left to share the third.

By the time they were done unpacking, the dressers and nightstands of Simon's side of the room were covered in glass tanks. A few were filled with fish. The rest were crammed with mice, lizards, and other animals that Simon had confined to mud-furnished cages. Their mother

had told Simon he could bring everything but the mice. She thought they were disgusting because Simon had rescued them from a trap in Mrs. Levette's downstairs apartment. She pretended not to notice he'd brought them anyway.

Jared tossed and turned on the lumpy mattress, pressing the pillow down over his head like he was smothering himself, but he couldn't sleep. He didn't mind sharing a room with Simon, but sharing a room with cages of animals that rustled, squeaked, and scratched was eerier than sleeping alone would have been. It made him think of the thing in the walls. He'd shared a room with Simon and the critters in the city, but the animal noises had dimmed against the background of cars and sirens and people. Here, everything was unfamiliar.

The creak of hinges startled him into jerking upright. There was a figure in the doorway, with a shapeless white gown and long, dark hair. Jared slid off the bed so fast he didn't even remember doing it.

"It's just me," the figure whispered. It was Mallory in a nightgown. "I think I heard your squirrel."

Jared stood up from a crouch, trying to decide if moving so fast meant he was a chicken or if he just had good reflexes. Simon was snoring gently in the other bed.

Mallory put her hands on her hips. "Come on. It's not going to wait around for us to catch it."

Jared shook his twin's shoulder. "Simon. Wake up. New pet. New peeeeeeeeet."

Simon twitched and groaned, trying to pull the covers over his head.

Mallory laughed.

"Simon." Jared leaned in close, making his voice deliberately urgent. "Squirrel! Squirrel!"

Simon opened his eyes and glared at them. "I was sleeping."

"Mom went out to the store for milk and cereal," Mallory said, pulling the covers off him. "She said I was supposed to keep an eye on you. We don't have much time before she gets back."

The three siblings crept along the dark hallways of their new house. Mallory was in the lead, walking a few paces and then stopping to listen. Every now and then there would be a scratch or a sound like small footsteps inside the walls.

The scuttling grew louder as they neared the kitchen. In the kitchen sink, Jared could see a pan crusted with the remains of the macaroni and cheese they'd had for dinner.

"I think it's there. Listen," Mallory whispered.

The sound stopped completely.

Mallory picked up a broom and held the wooden end like a baseball bat. "I'm going to knock open the wall," she said.

"Mom is going to see the hole when she gets back," Jared said.

"In this house? She'll never notice."

"What if you hit the squirrel?" Simon asked. "You could hurt—"

"Shhhh," Mallory said. She padded across the floor in her bare feet and swung the broom handle at the wall. The blow broke through the plaster, scattering dust like flour. It settled in Mallory's hair, making her look even more ghostly. She reached into the hole and broke off a chunk of the wall.

Jared stepped closer. He could feel the hair on his arms stand up.

Torn strips of cloth had been wadded up between the boards. As she snapped off more pieces, other things were revealed. The remains of curtains. Bits of tattered silk and lace. Straight pins poked into the wooden beams on either side, making a strange upward-snaking line. A doll's head lolled in one corner. Dead cockroaches were strung up like garlands. Tiny lead soldiers with melted hands and feet were scattered across the planks like a fallen army.

"I'm going to knock open the wall."

Jagged pieces of mirror glittered from where they had been glued with ancient gum.

Mallory reached into the nest and took out a fencing medal. It was silver with a thick blue ribbon. "This is mine."

"The squirrel must have stolen it," said Simon.

"No—this is too weird," Jared said.

"Dianna Beckley had ferrets, and they used to steal her Barbie dolls," Simon replied. "And lots of animals like shiny things."

"But look." Jared pointed to the cockroaches. "What ferret makes his own gross knickknacks?"

"Let's pull this stuff out of here," Mallory

said. "Maybe if it doesn't have a nest, it will be easier to keep out of the house."

Jared hesitated. He didn't want to put his hands inside the wall and feel around. What if it was still in there and bit him? Maybe he didn't know much, but he really didn't think squirrels were normally this creepy. "I don't think we should do that," he said.

Mallory wasn't listening. She was busy dragging over a trash can. Simon started pulling out wads of the musty cloth.

"There's no droppings, either. That's strange." Simon dumped what he was holding and pulled out another handful. At the army men, he stopped. "These are cool, aren't they, Jared?"

Jared had to nod. "They'd be better with hands, though."

Simon put several in the pocket of his pajamas.

"Simon?" Jared asked. "Have you ever heard of an animal like this? I mean, some of this stuff is really odd, you know? Like this squirrel must be as demented as Aunt Lucy."

"Yeah, it's real nutty," Simon said, and giggled.

Mallory groaned, then suddenly went quiet. "I hear it again."

"What?" Jared asked.

"The noise. Shhhh. It's over there." Mallory picked up the broom again.

"Quiet," Simon whispered.

"We're being quiet," Mallory hissed back.

"Shush," Jared said.

The three of them crept over to where the sound came from, just as the noise itself changed. Instead of hearing the clatter of little claws scrabbling on wood, they could clearly hear the scrape of nails on metal.

"Look." Simon bent down to touch a small sliding door set into the wall.

"It's a dumbwaiter," Mallory said. "Servants used it to send trays of breakfast and stuff upstairs. There must be another door like this in one of the bedrooms."

"That thing sounds like it's in the shaft," Jared said.

Mallory leaned her whole body into the metal box. "It's too small for me. One of you is going to have to go."

Simon looked at her skeptically. "I don't know. What if the ropes aren't that good anymore?"

"It would just be a short fall," Mallory said, and both the boys looked at her in astonishment.

"Oh, fine, I'll go." Jared was pleased to find something Mallory couldn't do. She looked a little bit put out. Simon just looked worried.

The inside was dirty and it smelled like old wood. Jared folded his legs in and bent his head forward. He fit, but only barely.

"Is the squirrel-thing even still in the dumbwaiter shaft?" Simon's voice sounded tinny and distant.

"I don't know," Jared said softly, listening to the echoes of his words. "I don't hear anything."

Mallory pulled the rope. With a little jolt and some shaking, the dumbwaiter began to move Jared up inside the wall. "Can you see anything?"

"No," Jared called. He could hear the

scratching sound, but it was distant. "It's completely black."

Mallory winched the dumbwaiter back down. "There's got to be a light around here somewhere." She opened a few drawers until she found the stub of a white candle and a mason jar. Turning a knob on the stove, she lit the wick off one of the gas burners, dripped hot wax into the jar, and pressed the candle against it to hold it in place. "Here, Jared. Hold this."

"Mallory, I don't even hear the thing anymore," said Simon.

"Maybe it's hiding," said Mallory, and yanked on the rope.

Jared tried to tuck himself deeper into the dumbwaiter, but there was no room. He wanted to tell them that this was stupid and that he'd chickened out, but he said nothing. Instead, he let himself be raised into the darkness, holding the makeshift lantern.

The metal box went up a few feet inside the wall. The light from the candle was a small halo, reflecting things erratically. The squirrel-thing could have been right next to him, almost touching him, and he would not have noticed it.

"I don't see anything," he called down, but he wasn't sure if anyone heard him.

The ascent was slow. Jared felt like he couldn't breathe. His knees were pressing against his chest, and his feet were cramping from being bent so long. He wondered if the candle was sucking up all the available oxygen.

Then, with a jerk, the dumbwaiter stopped. Something scraped against the metal box.

"It won't go any farther," Mallory called up the chute. "Do you see anything?"

The dumbwaiter began to move.

Jared wasn't sure where he was.

"No," said Jared. "I think it's stuck."

There was more scraping now, as though something was trying to claw through the top of the dumbwaiter. Jared yelped and tried to pound from the inside, hoping to frighten it off.

Just as suddenly, the dumbwaiter slid up an extra few feet and came to a halt again, this time in a room dimly lit by moonlight from a single, small window.

Jared scrambled out of the box. "I made it! I'm upstairs."

The room had a low ceiling, and the walls were covered in bookshelves. Looking around, he realized there was no door.

All of a sudden, Jared wasn't sure where he was.

Jared looked around the room.

Chapter Three

IN WHICH There Are Many Riddles

Jared looked around the room. It was a smallish library, with one huge desk in the center. On it was an open book and a pair of old-fashioned, round glasses that caught the candlelight. Jared walked closer. The dim glow illuminated one title at a time as he scanned the shelves. They were all strange: *A Historie of Scottish Dwarves, A Compendium of Brownie Visitations from Around the World,* and *Anatomy of Insects and Other Flying Creatures.*

A collection of glass jars containing berries,

dried plants, and one filled with dull river stones sat at the edge of the desk. Nearby, a watercolor sketch showed a little girl and a man playing on the lawn. Jared's eyes fell on a note tossed on top of an open book, both coated in a thin layer of dust. The paper was yellowed with age, but handwritten on it was a strange little poem:

In a man's torso you will find
My secret to all mankind
If false and true can be the same
You will soon know of my fame
Up and up and up again
Good luck dear friend

He picked it up and read it through carefully. It was as though a message had been left here just for him. But by whom? What did the poem mean?

He heard a shout from downstairs. "Mallory! Simon! What are you doing up?"

Jared groaned. It just figured that Mom would get back from the store *now*.

"There was a squirrel in the wall," Jared could hear Mallory say.

Their mother cut her off. "Where's Jared?"

Neither of his siblings said anything.

"You bring that dumbwaiter down. If your brother is in there . . ."

Jared ran over in time to watch the box disappear down into the wall. His candle choked on wax and sputtered from his sudden movement, but it didn't go out.

"See?" Simon said weakly.

The dumbwaiter must have showed up, empty.

"Well, where is he then?"

"I don't know," Mallory said. "In bed, asleep?"

Their mother sighed. "Well, go on, both of you, and join him. Now!"

Jared listened to their retreating steps. They'd have to wait a while before they snuck back down to get him. That is, if they didn't just figure that the dumbwaiter had taken him all the way upstairs. They'd probably be surprised *not* to find him in bed. How could they know he was trapped in a room without a door?

There was a rustling behind him. Jared spun around. It came from the desk.

As he held up the makeshift lamp, Jared saw that something had been scrawled in the dust of the desk. Something that wasn't there before.

Click clack, watch your back.

Jared jumped, causing his candle to tilt. Running wax snuffed the flame. He stood in the darkness, so scared he could barely move. Something was here, in the room, and it could write!

He backed toward the empty chute, biting the inside of his lip to keep from screaming. He could hear the rustling of bags downstairs as his mother unpacked groceries.

"What are you?"

"What's there?" he whispered into the darkness. "What are you?"

Only silence answered him.

"I know you're there," Jared said.

But there was no reply and no more rustling.

Then he heard his mother on the stairs, a door, and nothing. Nothing but a silence so thick and heavy that it choked him. He felt that even breathing too loudly would give him away. Any moment the thing would be upon him.

There was a creak from inside the wall. Startled, Jared dropped the jar, then realized it was only the dumbwaiter. He felt his way through the darkness.

"Get in," his sister whispered up the shaft.

Jared squeezed into the metal box. He was so filled with relief that he barely noticed the ride down to the kitchen.

As soon as he got out, he started speaking.

"There was a library! A secret library with weird books. And something was in there—it wrote in the dust."

"*Shhhh,* Jared," Simon said. "Mom's going to hear us."

Jared held up the piece of paper with the poem on it. "Look at this. It has some kind of directions on it."

"Did you actually *see* anything?" Mallory asked.

"I saw the message in the dust. It said 'watch your back,'" Jared replied hotly.

Mallory shook her head. "That could have been written there ages ago."

"It wasn't," Jared insisted. "I saw the desk and there was nothing written there before."

"Calm down," Mallory said.

"Mallory, I saw it!"

Mallory grabbed his shirt in her fist. "Be quiet!"

"Mallory! Let go of your brother!" Their mother was standing at the top of the narrow kitchen stairs wearing a less-than-pleased expression. "I thought we already went through this. If I see any of you out of your beds, I am going to lock you in your rooms."

Mallory let go of Jared's shirt with a long glare.

"What if we need to go to the bathroom?" Simon asked.

"Just go to bed," their mother said.

When they got upstairs, Jared and Simon went off to their room. Jared pulled the covers over his head and scrunched his eyes shut.

"I believe you . . . about the note and all," Simon whispered, but Jared didn't reply. He was just glad to be in bed. He thought he could probably stay there for a whole week.

"Just chop it."

Chapter Four

IN WHICH There Are Answers, Although Not Necessarily to the Right Questions

Jared woke up to the sound of Mallory's screaming. He jumped out of bed and rushed down the hall, past Simon, and into his sister's room. Long pieces of her hair had been knotted to the brass headboard. Her face was red, but the worst part was the strange pattern of bruises that decorated her arms. Their mother was seated on the mattress, her fingers tugging at the knots.

"What happened?" Jared asked.

"Just chop it," Mallory sobbed. "Cut it off.

I want to get out of this bed! I want out of this house! I hate this place!"

"Who did this?" Their mother looked at Jared angrily.

"I don't know!" Jared glanced at Simon standing in the doorway, looking puzzled. It must have been the thing in the walls.

Their mother's eyes got huge. It was scary. "Jared Grace, I saw you arguing with your sister last night!"

"Mom, I didn't do it. Honest." He was shocked that she thought he would do something like this. He and Mallory were always fighting, but it didn't mean anything.

"Get the scissors, Mom!" Mallory yelled.

"Both of you. Out. Jared, I will talk to you later." Mrs. Grace turned back to her daughter.

Jared left the room, his heart pounding. When he thought about Mallory's knotted hair, he couldn't contain a shiver.

"You think that thing did it, don't you?" Simon asked as they entered the bedroom.

Jared looked at his brother in dismay. "Don't you?"

Simon nodded.

"I keep thinking about that poem I found," Jared said. "It's the only clue we have."

"How is a stupid poem going to help?"

"I don't know." Jared sighed. "You're the

smart one. You should be figuring this out."

"How come nothing happened to us? Or to Mom?"

Jared hadn't even thought about that. "I don't know," he said again.

Simon gave him a long look.

"Well? What do *you* think?" Jared asked.

Simon started out the door. "I don't know what I think. I'm going to go try and catch some crickets."

Jared watched him go and wondered what he could do. Could he really solve anything by himself?

Getting dressed, he thought about the poem. "Up and up and up again" was the simplest line, but what did it mean exactly? Up in the house? Up on the roof? Up in a tree? Maybe the poem was just something that an old, dead relative was keeping around—

something that wasn't going to help at all.

But since Simon was feeding his animals and Mallory was being freed from her bed, he had nothing better to do than wonder how far "up and up and up again" he needed to go.

So, okay. Maybe it wasn't the easiest clue after all. But Jared figured it couldn't hurt to go up, past the second floor, to the attic.

The stairs were worn clean of their paint, and several times the boards he stepped on creaked so dramatically that Jared was afraid they were going to snap from his weight.

The attic level was a vast room with a slanted ceiling and a gaping hole in the floor on one end. Through it, he could see down into one of the unusable bedrooms.

Old garment bags hung from a clothesline of thin wire stretching across the width of the attic. Birdhouses hung in profusion from the rafters, and a dressmaker's dummy stood alone in a corner, a hat over its knobbed head. And in the center of the room, there was a spiral staircase.

Up and up and up again. Jared took the stairs two at a time.

Up and up and up again

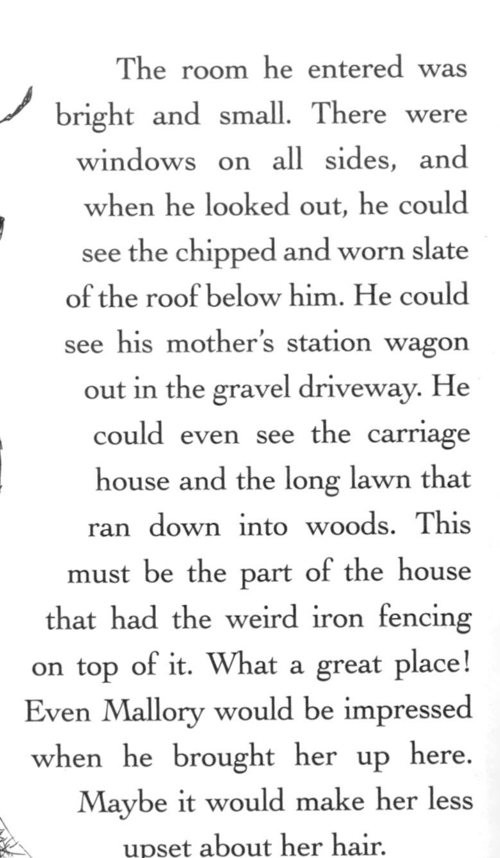

The room he entered was bright and small. There were windows on all sides, and when he looked out, he could see the chipped and worn slate of the roof below him. He could see his mother's station wagon out in the gravel driveway. He could even see the carriage house and the long lawn that ran down into woods. This must be the part of the house that had the weird iron fencing on top of it. What a great place! Even Mallory would be impressed when he brought her up here. Maybe it would make her less upset about her hair.

There wasn't much in

In a man's torso
you will find

My secret
to all mankind

If false and true
can be the same

You will soon know
of my fame

Up and up and up
again

Good luck dear friend

Handwritten note uncovered by Jared Grace in Arthur Spiderwick's upstairs library the room. An old trunk, a small stool, a Victrola, and rolls of faded fabric.

Jared sat down, pulled the crumpled poem from his pocket, and read it through again. "In a man's torso, you will find my secret to all mankind." Those lines bothered him. He didn't want to find an old, dead body, even if there was something really cool inside it.

The bright yellow sunlight splashing across the floor reassured him. In movies, bad things seldom happened in broad daylight, but he still hesitated to open the trunk.

Maybe he should go outside and get Simon to come up with him. But what if the chest was empty? Or what if the poem had nothing to do with Mallory's bruises and knotted hair?

Not knowing what else to do, he knelt down and brushed cobwebs and grime from the top of the trunk. Heavy strips of rusted metal striped the rotting leather. At least he could take a look. Maybe the clue would be more obvious if he knew what was inside.

Taking a breath, Jared pushed up the lid. It was full of very old, moth-eaten clothes. Underneath, there was a pocket watch on a long chain, a tattered cap, and a leather satchel full of old, odd-looking pencils and cracked bits of charcoal.

Nothing in the trunk looked like it was a secret, for mankind or anybody else.

Nothing looked like a dead body, either.

"In a man's torso, you will find my secret to all mankind."

He looked down at the contents of the chest again, and it hit him.

He was looking at a *chest.* A man's torso would be his *chest.*

Jared groaned in frustration. How could he

be right and still have nothing to show for it? There was nothing good in the chest, and the other lines of the poem made no sense at all. "If false and true can be the same, you will soon know of my fame." How could that be answered with something real? It sounded like a word game.

What could be false, though? Something about this situation? Something about the stuff

in the chest? The chest itself? He thought about chests, and chests made him think about pirates on a beach, burying treasure deep in the cool sand.

Buried underneath! Not a false chest, but a chest with a false bottom! Looking carefully, he could see that the inside seemed higher than it should be. Had he really solved the riddle?

Jared got down on his knees and began to push all over the floor of the trunk, threading his fingers through the dust to look for seams that might allow him to pull an unseen compartment open. When he found nothing, he began to touch the outside, pawing over the box. Finally, when he pressed three fingers against the edge of the left side, a compartment popped open.

Excited beyond reason, Jared pressed his

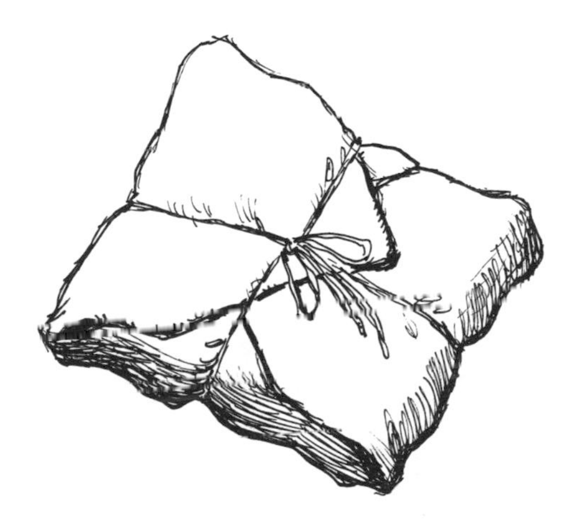

hand inside. The only contents were a squarish bundle, wrapped in a dirty cloth. He took it out, untied it, and started to unfold the fabric from an old, crumbling book that smelled like burnt paper. Embossed on the brown leather, the title read: *Arthur Spiderwick's Field Guide to the Fantastical World Around You.*

The cover was ragged at the edges, and as he opened it, he noticed that it was full of watercolor sketches. The writing had been

The strangest thing

done in ink, grown smudged and spotted with age and water damage. He flipped the pages quickly, glancing at notes tucked into the volume. These were written in a spidery hand very like the writing of the riddle.

The strangest thing, however, was the subject matter. The book was full of information about faeries.

He just wanted to keep reading.

Chapter Five

IN WHICH Jared Reads a Book and Sets a Trap

Mallory and Simon were out on the lawn, fencing, when Jared found them. Mallory's ponytail stuck out of the back of her fencing helmet, and Jared could see that it was shorter than it had once been. She was apparently trying to make up for her earlier weakness by ruthless fencing. Simon couldn't seem to get a strike in at all. He was being backed against the side of the broken-down carriage house, his parries becoming increasingly desperate.

"I found something!" Jared called.

Simon turned his helmeted head. Mallory took that opportunity to strike, pushing the rubber tip of her fencing foil against his chest.

"That's three to zip," Mallory said. "I creamed you."

"You cheated," he complained.

"You allowed yourself to become distracted," Mallory countered.

Simon pulled the helmet off his head, flung it down, and looked at Jared. "Thanks a lot."

"Sorry," Jared said automatically.

"You're the one that always fences with her. I just came out here to catch tadpoles." Simon scowled.

"Well, I was busy. Just because I don't have a bunch of dumb animals to take care of doesn't mean I can't be busy," Jared shot back.

"Just shut up, both of you." Mallory took off her own helmet. Her face was flushed. "What did you find?"

Jared tried to recapture some of his earlier excitement. "A book in the attic. It's about faeries, real faeries. Look, they're ugly."

Mallory took the book out of his hands and looked it over. "This is baby stuff. A storybook."

"It's not," Jared said defensively. "It's a *field guide*. You know, like for birds. So you know how to spot the different kinds."

"You think a *faerie* tied my hair to my bed?"

Mallory asked. "Mom thinks you did. She thinks you've been acting weird ever since Dad left. Like getting into all those fights at school."

Simon didn't say anything.

"But *you* don't think that." Jared hoped she would agree. "And you *always* get into fights."

Mallory took a deep breath. "I don't think you're stupid enough to have done it," she said, holding up a fist to show what she was going to do to whatever had. "But I don't think it was faeries, either."

Over dinner, their mother was oddly quiet as she slid chicken and mashed potatoes onto their plates. Mallory wasn't talking that much either, but Simon was going on and on about the tadpoles he had found and how they were going to be frogs in no time because they already had little arms.

Jared had seen them. They had a long way to go. What Simon called arms looked a lot more like fish zits.

"Mom?" Jared said finally. "Do we have a relative named Arthur?"

Their mother looked up suspiciously from her dinner. "No. I don't think so. Why do you ask?"

"I was just wondering," Jared mumbled. "What about Spiderwick?"

"That's your great-aunt Lucinda's surname," his mother said. "It was my mother's maiden name. Maybe Arthur was one of her relatives. Now, tell me why you want to know all this?"

"I just found some of his stuff in the attic—that's all," Jared said.

"In the attic!" His mother almost spilled her iced tea. "Jared Grace, as you know, half of the entire second floor is so rotted that if you step wrong, you'll find yourself in the downstairs parlor."

"I stayed on the safe side," Jared protested.

"We don't know if there is a safe side in the attic. I don't want anyone playing up there, especially you," she said, looking right at Jared.

He bit his lip. *Especially you.* Jared didn't say a thing for the rest of dinner.

"Are you going to read that all night?" Simon asked. He was sitting on his side of the room. Jeffrey and Lemondrop were running around on the comforter, and his new tadpoles were set up in one of the fish tanks.

"So what if I do?" Jared asked. With each crumbling page, Jared was learning strange facts. Could there really be brownies in his house? Pixies in his yard? Nixies in the stream out back? The book made them so real. He didn't want to talk to anyone right now, not even Simon. He just wanted to keep reading.

"I don't know," Simon said. "I thought maybe you'd be bored by now. You don't usually like to read."

Jared looked up and blinked. It was true. Simon was the reader. Jared mostly just got into trouble.

He turned a page. "I can read if I want to."

Simon yawned. "Are you worried about

falling asleep? I mean about what might happen tonight."

"Look at this." Jared flipped to a page close to the front. "There's this faerie called a brownie—"

"Like Girl Scouts?"

"I don't know," Jared said. "Like this. Look." He pushed the page in front of Simon. On the yellowed paper was an ink drawing of a little man, posed with a feather duster made from a badminton birdie and a straight pin. Next to it was a hunched figure, also small, but this one held a piece of broken glass.

"What's with that?" Simon pointed to the second figure, intrigued despite himself.

"This Arthur guy says it's a boggart. See, brownies are these helpful guys, but then if you make them mad, they go crazy. They start doing all these bad things and you can't stop

"Look at this."

them. Then they become boggarts. That's what I think we have."

"You think we made it mad by messing up its house?"

"Yeah, maybe. Or maybe it was kind of wacky before that. I mean, look at this guy"—Jared pointed to the brownie—"he's not the type to live in a skeevy house decorated with dead bugs."

Simon nodded, looking at the pictures. "Since you found the book in this house," he said, "do you think that this is a picture of *our* boggart?"

"I never thought of that," Jared said quietly. "It makes sense, though."

"Does it say in the book what we should do?"

Jared shook his head. "It talks about different ways to catch it. Not catch it for real, but see it . . . or get evidence."

"Jared." Simon sounded doubtful. "Mom

From the Field Guide

said to close the door and stay in here. The last thing she needs is another reason to believe that you were the one that attacked Mallory."

"But she thinks it was me anyway. If something happens tonight, she'll think it was me too."

"She won't. I'll tell her you were here all night. And besides, that way we can make sure nothing happens to either one of us."

"What about Mallory?" Jared asked.

Simon shrugged. "I saw her getting into bed with one of her fencing swords. I wouldn't mess with her."

"Yeah." Jared got into bed and opened the book again. "I'm just going to read a little more."

Simon nodded and got up to put the mice back in their tanks. Then he got into bed and pulled the covers over his head with a mumbled "good night."

As Jared read, each page took him deeper

into the strange world of forest and stream, alive with creatures that seemed so close that he could almost stroke the slick, scaly flanks of the mermaids. He could almost feel the heat of the troll's breath and hear the rumble of the dwarven forges.

When he turned the last page, it was late at night. Simon was bundled up so that Jared could see only the top of his head. Jared listened hard, but the only sounds in the house were the wind whistling through the roof above them and water gurgling through the pipes. No scuttling or screaming. Even Simon's beasts were asleep.

Jared flipped to the page that read, *Boggarts delight in tormenting those they once protected and will cause milk to sour, doors to slam, dogs to go lame, and other malicious mischief.*

Simon believed him—sort of, anyway—but Mallory and their mom wouldn't. And besides, he and Simon were twins. It almost didn't count for anything that Simon believed him. Jared looked at the suggestion of the book: *Scattering sugar or flour on the floor is one way of obtaining footprints.*

If he had footprints to show, then they'd have to believe him.

Jared opened the door and crept downstairs. It was dark in the kitchen and everything was quiet. He tiptoed across the cool tile to where his mother had put the flour—in an old glass apothecary jar on the countertop. He took out several handfuls and scattered them liberally on the floor. It didn't look like much. He wasn't sure how well footprints would show up in it.

Maybe the boggart wouldn't even walk across the kitchen floor. So far, it seemed to stick to moving through the walls. He thought about what he knew about boggarts from the

Everything was quiet.

book. Malicious. Hateful. Hard to get rid of.

In their brownie form they were helpful and nice. They did all kinds of work for a plain old bowl of milk. Maybe . . . Jared went over to the fridge and poured milk into a small saucer. Maybe if he left it out, the creature would be tempted to come out of the walls and leave footprints in the flour.

But when he looked at the saucer of milk there on the floor, he couldn't help feeling a little bit bad and a little bit weird at the same time. In the first place, it was weird that he was down here, setting a trap for something that he didn't even know if he would have believed in two weeks ago.

But the reason he felt bad was . . . well, he knew what it was like to be mad, and he knew how easy it was to get into a fight, even if you were really mad at someone else. And he thought that just maybe that was how the boggart felt.

But then he noticed something else. He'd left footprints of his own in the flour all the way from the milk back to the hall.

"Crud," he muttered as he went to get the broom. The light cracked on.

"Jared Grace!" It was his mother's voice, coming from the top of the stairs.

Jared turned fast, but he knew how guilty he looked.

"Get back to bed," she said.

"I was just trying to catch—" But she didn't let him finish.

"Now, mister. Go."

After he thought about it for a minute, he was glad she'd interrupted him. His boggart idea probably wouldn't have been a big hit.

With a look back over his shoulder at the flour dusting the floor, Jared slunk up the stairs.

The kitchen was a mess.

Chapter Six

IN WHICH They Find Unexpected Things in the Icebox

Jared rolled over at the sound of his mother's voice. She was angry. "Jared, you better get up."

"What's going on?" Jared asked sleepily, peering up from the covers. For a second he thought he'd missed school, until he remembered they'd moved and not even so much as set foot in the new school yet.

"Up, Jared!" his mother said. "You want to pretend you don't know? Fine, let's go downstairs so you can *see* what's going on."

The kitchen was a mess. Mallory had a

broom and was sweeping up broken pieces of a porcelain bowl. The walls were painted with chocolate syrup and orange juice. Raw eggs oozed down the windowpanes.

Simon was sitting at the kitchen table. His arms were covered with the same bruises Mallory had been wearing only a day before, and his eyes were red-rimmed, like he'd been crying.

"Well?" his mother asked expectantly.

"I—I didn't do this," Jared said, looking around at them. They couldn't really believe he would do something like this, could they?

And there, on the floor of the kitchen, next to drifts of cereal and scattered pieces of orange peel, Jared saw small tracks in the flour. They were the size of his little finger, and he could clearly see the imprint of the heel of a foot and a feathering in the front that might have been from toes.

"Look," Jared said, pointing. "See. Little footprints."

Mallory looked up at him, and her eyes were narrowed with fury. "Just shut up, Jared. Mom says she saw you down here last night. You made those footprints!"

"I did not!" Jared yelled back.

"Why don't you look in the freezer then, huh?"

"What?" Jared asked.

Simon gave an especially wet-sounding sob.

Their mother took the broom from Mallory's hand and started sweeping up the flour and cereal.

"Mom, no, the footprints," Jared said, but

his mother didn't pay any attention to him. Two strokes of the broom, and the only proof he had was swept into a pile of rubbish.

Mallory opened the freezer door. Each of Simon's tadpoles was frozen into a single cube in the tray. Next to them was a note written in ink on a piece of a cereal box:

Not very nice to ice the mice.

"And Jeffrey and Lemondrop are gone!" said Simon.

"Now, why don't you tell us what you did with your brother's mice?" said his mother.

"Mom, I didn't do it. I really didn't."

Mallory gripped Jared by the shoulder. "I don't know what you think you're doing, but you're about to start regretting it."

"Mallory," their mother cautioned. His sister

"Mom, I didn't do it."

let go, but the look she gave him carried the promise of later violence.

"I don't think Jared did it," said Simon, between sniffs. "I think it was the boggart."

Their mother said nothing. The look on her face said that manipulating Simon was the worst thing Jared had done. "Jared," she said, "start taking this trash out to the front. If you thought this was funny, let's see how funny you think it is when you spend the rest of today cleaning it up."

Jared hung his head. He had no way of making her believe him. Silently, he got dressed, then gathered up three black garbage bags and started dragging them toward the front of the house.

Outside, the weather was warm and the sky was blue. The air smelled of pine needles and freshly mown grass. But daylight didn't seem to be any comfort at all.

One of the bags snagged on a branch, and when Jared tugged, the plastic ripped. Groaning, he dropped the bags and surveyed the damage. The tear was large, and most of the garbage had spilled out. As he started to gather things up, he realized what he was holding. The contents of the creature's house!

He looked at the worn bits of cloth, the doll's head, and the pins with pearl tops. In the daylight there were other things he had not noticed before. There had been a robin's egg, but it was crushed. Tiny slips of newspaper were scattered throughout, each one with a different strange word on it. "Luminous," read one. "Soliloquy," read another.

Gathering up all the pieces of the nest, Jared put them carefully aside from the rest of the trash. Could he make a new house for the boggart? Would it matter? Could that stop it?

He thought about Simon crying and about the poor, stupid tadpoles frozen in ice cubes. He didn't want to help the boggart. He wanted to catch it and kick it and make it sorry it ever came out of the wall.

Dragging the rest of the bags to the front lawn, he looked at the pile of the boggart's things. Still not sure whether he was going to burn them or give them back or what, he carried them inside.

His mother was standing in the doorway waiting for him. "What's all that?" she asked.

"Nothing," Jared said.

For once, she didn't question him. At least not about the junk pile in his hands.

"Jared, I know you're upset about your father leaving. We're all upset."

Jared looked at his shoes in discomfort. Just because he was upset about his father

There were other strange things.

leaving did not mean he had trashed their new house, or pinched his brother black and blue, or tied his sister's hair to her headboard. "So?" he asked, thinking that her silence meant she was waiting for a response.

"So?" she repeated. "*So* you need to stop letting your anger control you, Jared Grace. Your sister works things out when she's fencing and your brother has his animals, but you . . ."

"I didn't do it," Jared said. "Why won't you believe me? Is it because of the fight at school?"

"I have to admit," his mother said, "I was shocked to learn that you broke a boy's nose. That is just the kind of thing I'm talking about. Simon doesn't get into fights. And neither did you before your father left."

He studied his shoes even more intently. "Can I go inside now?"

She nodded, but then she stopped him with one hand on his shoulder. "If anything else happens around here, I'm going to have to take you to see someone. Do you understand?"

Jared nodded, but he felt weird. He remembered what he had said about Aunt Lucy and the nuthouse and suddenly felt very, very sorry.

"Mallory, no!"

Chapter Seven

IN WHICH the Fate of the Mice Is Discovered

"I really need your help," said Jared. His brother and sister were lying on the rug in front of the television. Each one had a controller, and from where he was standing, he could see colors flit across their faces as the screen changed.

Mallory snorted but didn't reply. Jared took that as a positive response. At this point, anything that didn't involve fists was a positive response.

"I know you think I did it," Jared said,

opening the book to the page about boggarts. "But, honest, I didn't. You heard the thing in the walls. There was the writing on the desk and the footprints in the flour. And remember

the nest? Remember how you guys pulled everything out of that nest?"

Mallory stood up and snatched the book out of his hands.

"Give it back," Jared pleaded, making a grab for it.

Mallory held it over her head. "This book is what started all the trouble."

"No!" Jared said. "That's not true. I got the book *after* your hair was knotted. Give it back, Mallory. Please give it back."

Now she held it in two hands, one on either side of the open book, poised to rip it apart.

"Mallory, no! No!" Jared was nearly speechless with panic. If he didn't think of something quick, the book was going to be in pieces.

"Wait, Mal," Simon said, getting up from the floor.

Mallory waited.

"What help did you want, Jared?"

Jared took a deep breath. "I've been thinking that if our messing up the nest is what got it upset, then maybe we could make it a new nest. I—I took a birdhouse and put some stuff in it.

"I thought—well—I thought that maybe the boggart was a little bit like us, because it's stuck here too. I mean, maybe it doesn't even want to be here. Maybe being here makes it mad."

"Okay, before I say I believe you," Mallory said, holding the book in a less threatening position, "tell me *exactly* what you want us to do."

"I need you guys to work the dumbwaiter," Jared said, "so I can bring the house up to the library. I thought it would be safe there."

"Let's see this house," Mallory said. She and Simon followed Jared into the hall, and he showed it to them.

It was made from a wooden birdhouse large enough for a crow to roost in. Jared had found it among the ones hung in the attic. Sliding up the back, he showed them how he had arranged everything except the cockroaches neatly inside. On the walls, he had taped up the newspaper words and also a few small pictures from magazines.

"Did you cut up Mom's stuff to make that?" Simon asked.

"Yeah," Jared said, and shrugged.

"You really did a lot of work," Mallory said.

"So you'll help me?" Jared

wanted to ask for the book back, but he didn't want to make his sister mad all over again.

Mallory looked at Simon and nodded.

"I want to go first, though," said Simon.

Jared hesitated. "Sure," he said.

Walking quietly past the den where their mother was phoning construction people, they went into the kitchen.

Simon hesitated in front of the dumbwaiter. "Do you think my mice are alive?"

Jared didn't know what to say. He thought about the tadpoles, frozen in ice. He wanted Simon to help but didn't want to lie.

Simon got down on his knees and climbed into the dumbwaiter. In a few moments, Mallory had wheeled him up inside the wall. Simon gave a small gasp as he started moving, but then they heard nothing, even after the dumbwaiter stopped.

"You said there was a desk in there and papers," Mallory said.

"Yeah." Jared wasn't sure what she was driving at. If she didn't believe him, she could ask Simon when he came back down.

"Well, they needed to get it in there somehow. And it wasn't little, right? So an adult worked in there—but how did an adult get in there?"

Jared was puzzled for a moment, then he understood. "A secret door?"

Mallory nodded. "Maybe."

The dumbwaiter came back down and Jared got inside, the little house cradled in his lap. Mallory winched him up inside the dark tunnel. The trip was fast, but he was still very, very glad to see the library.

Simon was standing in the middle of the room, looking around in awe.

Jared grinned. "See?"

"It's so cool in here," said Simon. "Look at all these animal books."

Thinking about the secret door, Jared tried to picture where he must be in relation to the rest of the rooms upstairs. He figured which direction would head toward the hall.

"Mallory thinks there's a hidden door," Jared said.

Simon came over. There was a bookcase, a large picture, and a cabinet in front of the wall Jared was looking at.

"Picture," Simon said, and together they took down the large oil painting. It was of a thin man with glasses sitting stiffly on a green chair. Jared wondered if that was Arthur Spiderwick.

Behind the picture was nothing but flat wall.

"Maybe we could pull out some of the

"It's so cool in here."

books?" Jared said, taking out one entitled *Mysterious Mushrooms, Fabulous Fungi.*

Simon opened the cabinet doors. "Hey, look at this." They opened into the upstairs linen closet.

A few minutes later, Mallory was looking around the room too.

"This place is creepy," Mallory said.

Simon grinned. "Yeah, and no one knows about it but us."

"And the boggart," said Jared.

He hung his birdhouse from a wall sconce. Mallory and Simon helped him make sure that the insides were arranged, and then each of them added something to the house. Jared put in one of his winter gloves, thinking that the boggart could use it as a sleeping bag. Simon added a small dish he'd once used to give his lizards water. And Mallory must have believed

Jared a little, because she tucked her silver fencing medal with the blue ribbon neatly inside.

When they were done, they looked it over. They all thought it was a fine house.

"Let's leave it a note," Simon suggested.

"A note?" Jared asked.

"Yeah." Simon pawed through the drawers of the desk and found some paper, a pen with a nib, and a bottle of ink.

"Hey, I didn't notice this," Jared said. He pointed to the watercolor painting of a man and a little girl on the desk. Underneath it in faint pencil was the inscription "my darling daughter Lucinda, age 4."

"So Arthur was her dad?" Mallory asked.

"I guess so," said Simon, clearing space on the desk to write.

"Let me do it," Mallory said. "You guys will take forever. Just tell what to write." She unstoppered the ink and dipped the pen. It made a scratchy but legible line on the paper.

"Dear Boggart," Simon started.

"Do you think that's polite?" Jared asked.

"I already wrote it," Mallory said.

"Dear Boggart," Simon said again. "We are writing you to say that we are sorry we messed up your first house. We hope you like what we

made and that even if you don't, that you'll stop pinching us—and other things—and that if you have Jeffrey and Lemondrop to please take care of them because they are good mice."

"Got it," Mallory said.

"Okay, then," said Jared.

They put the note on the floor near the little house and left the library.

Over the next week, none of them had time to visit the library, even through the linen closet. Construction people and movers were milling around the house during the day, and their mother was watching them closely at night, even going so far as to pace the hallways.

School had finally started, which wasn't as bad as Jared had feared. The new school was small, but it had a fencing team for Mallory, and no one was too mean to them their first couple of days there. So far, Jared had managed to behave.

Best of all, there were no more night attacks, no more scuttling in the walls—nothing other than Mallory's shorter hair to make it seem like the whole thing had really happened.

Except that Simon and Mallory were as eager to visit the room again as Jared was.

They got their chance one Sunday, when their mother went out shopping and left Mallory in charge. As soon as their mom's car pulled out of the driveway, they rushed up to the closet.

Inside the library, very little had changed. The painting leaned up against the wall, the birdhouse hung from the sconce, everything appeared to be just the way they'd left it.

"The note's gone!" announced Simon.

"Did you take it?" Mallory asked Jared.

"No!" Jared insisted.

There was the loud sound of a throat being cleared, and the three turned toward the desk. Standing on it, in worn overalls and a wide-brimmed hat, was a little man about the size of a pencil. His eyes were as black as beetles, his nose was large and red, and he looked very like the illustration from the Guide. He was holding a pair of leashes that attached to two gray mice that were sniffing the edge of the desk.

"Jeffrey! Lemondrop!" Jared squealed.

"Thimbletack likes his new house well," the little man said, "but that's not what he's come to tell."

Jared nodded, not sure what to say. Mallory looked like someone had smacked her in the face but she hadn't figured it out yet.

The mannikin went on. "Arthur Spiderwick's book is not for your kind. Too much about Fey for a mortal to find. All who have kept it have come to harm. Be it through violence or through charm. Throw the book away, toss it in a fire. If you do not heed, you will draw their ire."

"They? Who are they?" Jared asked, but the little man just tipped his cap and jumped off the side of the desk. He landed in the bright flood of sunlight in the open window and disappeared.

Mallory seemed to break out of her trance. "Can I see the book?" she asked.

Jared nodded. He'd taken to keeping it with him wherever he went.

Mallory knelt down and flipped through the pages with her fingers, quicker than Jared could read.

"Hey," Jared said. "What are you doing?"

About the size of a pencil

"Throw the book away."

Mallory's voice was weird. "I was just looking. I mean—this is a big book."

It wasn't a *small* book. "Yeah, I guess."

"And all these entries . . . all these *things* are real? Jared, that's a lot of real."

And then, suddenly, Jared understood what she was saying. If you looked at it that way, it was a big book, an absolutely huge book, too large to even comprehend. And worst of all, they were only at the beginning.

About TONY DiTERLIZZI . . .

A *New York Times* best-selling author, Tony DiTerlizzi created the Zena Sutherland Award–winning *Ted, Jimmy Zangwow's Out-of-This-World Moon Pie Adventure,* as well as illustrations in Tony Johnston's Alien and Possum beginning-reader series. Most recently, his brilliantly cinematic version of Mary Howitt's classic *The Spider and the Fly* was awarded a Caldecott Honor. In addition, Tony's art has graced the work of such well-known fantasy names as J.R.R. Tolkien, Anne McCaffrey, Peter S. Beagle, and Greg Bear as well as Wizards of the Coast's *Magic The Gathering*. He and his wife, Angela, reside with their pug, Goblin, in Amherst, Massachusetts. Visit Tony on the World Wide Web at www.diterlizzi.com.

and HOLLY BLACK

An avid collector of rare folklore volumes, Holly Black spent her early years in a decaying Victorian mansion where her mother fed her a steady diet of ghost stories and books about faeries. Accordingly, her first novel, *Tithe: A Modern Faerie Tale,* is a gothic and artful glimpse at the world of Faerie. Published in the fall of 2002, it received two starred reviews and a Best Book for Young Adults citation from the American Library Association. She lives in West Long Branch, New Jersey, with her husband, Theo, and a remarkable menagerie. Visit Holly on the World Wide Web at www.blackholly.com.

Tony and Holly continue to work day and night fending off angry faeries and goblins in order to bring the Grace children's story to you.

You may know
the Grace kids well,
but there is still
much tale to tell. . . .

Like, who'd dare live
within a stream
beneath a bridge
where dark thoughts teem?

And where'd your
loose tooth really go?
To a friend?
Or to a foe?

Keep on reading,
and you will know.

ACKNOWLEDGMENTS

Tony and Holly would like to thank
Steve and Dianna for their insight,
Starr for her honesty,
Myles and Liza for sharing the journey,
Ellen and Julie for helping make this our reality,
Kevin for his tireless enthusiasm and faith in us,
and especially Angela and Theo—
there are not enough superlatives
to describe your patience
in enduring endless nights
of Spiderwick discussion.

The text type for this book is set in Cochin.
The display types are set in Nevins Hand and Rackham.
The illustrations are rendered in pen and ink.
Production editor: Dorothy Gribbin
Art director: Dan Potash
Production manager: Chava Wolin

All five goblins were circling them.

Tony DiTerlizzi *and* Holly Black

Simon and Schuster Books for Young Readers

New York London Toronto Sydney Singapore

SIMON & SCHUSTER BOOKS FOR YOUNG READERS
An imprint of Simon & Schuster Children's Publishing Division
1230 Avenue of the Americas, New York, New York 10020

 • Book design by Tony DiTerlizzi and Dan Potash • Manufactured in the United States of America

20 19

Library of Congress Cataloging-in-Publication Data
Black, Holly.
The seeing stone / Holly Black and Tony DiTerlizzi.
p. cm. — (Spiderwick chronicles ; 2)
Sequel to: The field guide.
Summary: When Mallory and Jared attempt to rescue Simon from goblins, they use a magical stone that enables them to see things that are normally invisible.
ISBN 0-689-85937-6
[1. Goblins—Fiction. 2. Brothers and sisters—Fiction. 3. Single-parent families—Fiction.] I. DiTerlizzi, Tony. II. Title.
III. Series.
PZ7.B52878 Go 2003
[Fic]—dc21
2002013523

For my grandmother, Melvina,
who said I should write a book just like this one
and to whom I replied that I never would
—H. B.

For Arthur Rackham,
may you continue to inspire others
as you have me
—T. D.

Table of
Contents

List of Full-Page
Illustrations

Dear Reader,

Over the years that Tony and I have been friends, we've shared the same childhood fascination with faeries. We did not realize the importance of that bond or how it might be tested.

One day Tony and I—along with several other authors—were doing a signing at a large bookstore. When the signing was over, we lingered, helping to stack books and chatting, until a clerk approached us. He said that there had been a letter left for us. When I inquired which one of us, we were surprised by his answer.

"Both of you," he said.

The letter was exactly as reproduced on the following page. Tony spent a long time just staring at the photocopy that came with it. Then, in a hushed voice, he wondered aloud about the remainder of the manuscript. We hurriedly wrote a note, tucked it back into the envelope, and asked the clerk to deliver it to the Grace children.

Not long after, a package arrived on my doorstep, bound in red ribbon. A few days after that, three children rang the bell and told me this story.

What has happened since is hard to describe. Tony and I have been plunged into a world we never quite believed in. We now see that faeries are far more than childhood stories. There is an invisible world around us and we hope that you, dear reader, will open your eyes to it.

HOLLY BLACK

Dear Mrs. Black and Mr. DiTerlizzi:

I know that a lot of people don't believe in faeries, but I do and I think that you do too. After I read your books, I told my brothers about you and we decided to write. We know about real faeries. In fact, we know a lot about them.

The page attached* to this one is a photocopy from an old book we found in our attic. It isn't a great copy because we had some trouble with the copier. The book tells people how to identify faeries and how to protect themselves. Can you please give this book to your publisher? If you can, please put a letter in this envelope and give it back to the store. We will find a way to send the book. The normal mail is too dangerous.

We just want people to know about this. The stuff that has happened to us could happen to anyone.

Sincerely,

Mallory, Jared, and Simon Grace

*Not included.

THE JUNKYARD
THE CAMP
THE BRIDGE
THE SPIDERWICK ESTATE
ROUNTREE STREET
DULAC DRIVE
THE GROVE

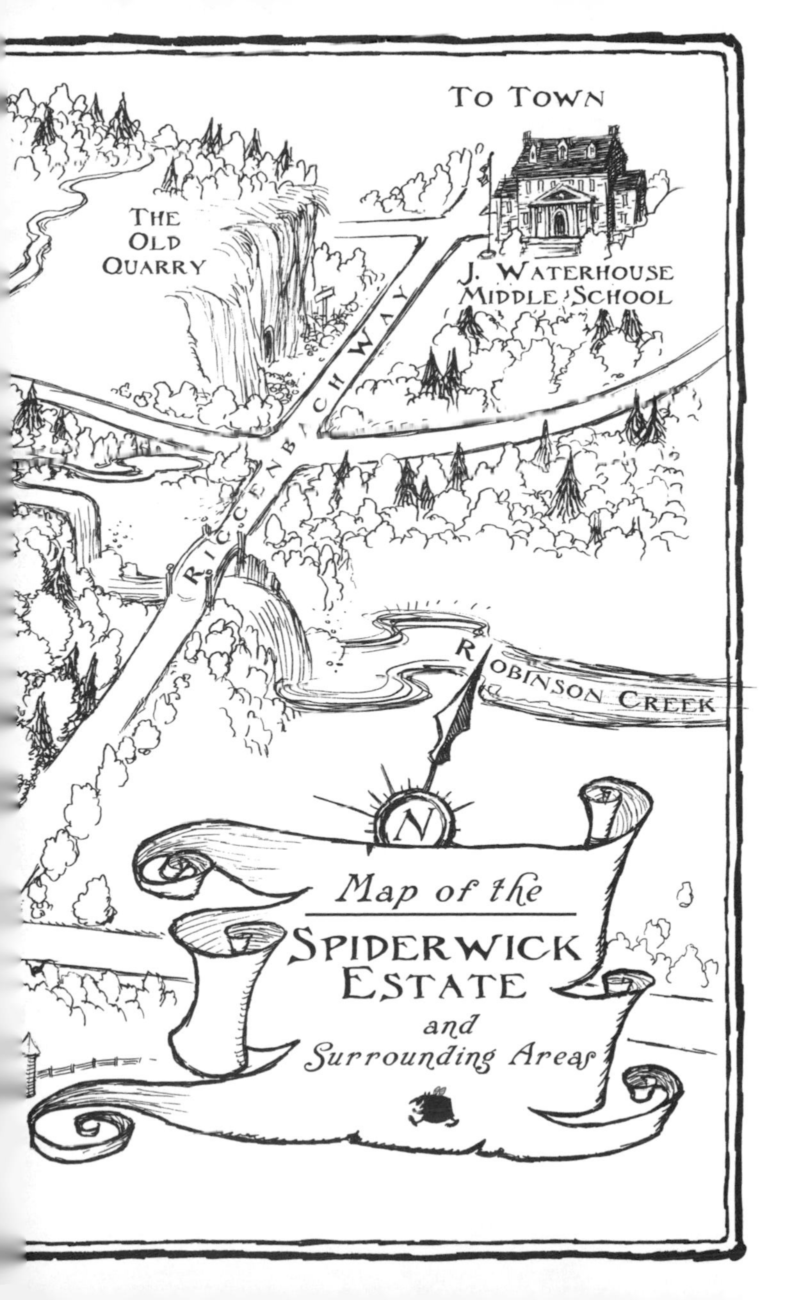

TO TOWN
THE OLD QUARRY
J. WATERHOUSE MIDDLE SCHOOL
RICCENBACH WAY
ROBINSON CREEK
N
Map of the
SPIDERWICK ESTATE
and
Surrounding Areas

THE
SPIDERWICK
CHRONICLES

The place looked as bad as Jared felt.

Chapter One

IN WHICH More Than a Cat Goes Missing

The late bus dropped Jared Grace at the bottom of his street. From there it was an uphill climb to the dilapidated old house where his family was staying until his mother found something better or his crazy old aunt wanted it back. The red and gold leaves of the low-hanging trees around the gate made the gray shingles look forlorn. The place looked as bad as Jared felt.

He couldn't believe he'd had to stay after school already.

It wasn't like he didn't try to get along with

the other kids. He just wasn't good at it. Take today, for example. Sure, he'd been drawing a brownie while the teacher was talking, but he was still paying attention. More or less. And she didn't have to hold up his drawing in front of the whole class. After that, the kids wouldn't stop bothering him. Before he knew it, he was ripping some boy's notebook in half.

He'd hoped things would be *better* at this school. But since his parents' divorce, things had gone from bad to worse.

Jared walked into the kitchen. His twin, Simon, sat at the old farmhouse table with an untouched saucer of milk in front of him.

Simon looked up. "Have you seen Tibbs?"

"I just got home." Jared went to the fridge and took a swig of apple juice. It was so cold that it made his head hurt.

"Well, did you see him *outside*?" Simon

asked. "I've looked everywhere."

Jared shook his head. He didn't care about the stupid cat. She was just the newest member of Simon's menagerie. One more animal wanting to be petted or fed, or jumping on his lap when he was busy.

Jared didn't know why he and Simon were so different. In movies, identical twins got cool powers like reading each other's minds with a look. It figured that the most real-life twins could do was wear the same-size pants.

Their sister, Mallory, thundered down the stairs, lugging a large bag. The hilts of fencing swords stuck out from one end.

"Hey, good job getting detention, nutcase." Mallory slung the bag over her shoulder and walked toward the back door. "At least this time, no one's nose got broken."

"Don't tell Mom, okay, Mal?" Jared pleaded.

"Whatever. She's going to find out sooner or later." Mallory shrugged and headed out onto the lawn. Clearly this new fencing team was even more competitive than the last. Mallory had taken to practicing at every spare moment. It bordered on obsessive.

"Hey, good job getting detention, nutcase."

"I'm going to Arthur's library," Jared said, and started up the stairs.

"But you have to help me find Tibbs. I waited for you to get home so you could help."

"I don't *have* to do anything." Jared took the stairs two at a time.

In the upstairs hall he opened the linen closet and went inside. Behind the stacks of mothball-packed, yellowed sheets was the door to the house's secret room.

It was dim, lit faintly by a single window, and had the musty smell of old dust. The walls were lined with crumbling books. A massive desk covered in old papers and glass jars dominated one side of the room. Great-Great-Uncle Arthur's secret library. Jared's favorite place.

He glanced back at the painting that hung next to the entrance. A portrait of Arthur Spiderwick peered down at him with small eyes

half hidden behind tiny, round glasses. Arthur didn't look that old, but he had a pinched mouth and he seemed stuffy. He certainly didn't seem like someone who would believe in faeries.

Opening the first drawer on the left-hand side of the desk, Jared tugged free a cloth-wrapped book: *Arthur Spiderwick's Field Guide to the Fantastical World Around You.* He'd only found it a few weeks before, but already Jared had come to think of it as *his*. He kept it with him most of the time, sometimes even sleeping with it under his pillow. He would have even brought it to school, but he was afraid someone would take it from him.

There was a faint sound inside the wall.

"Thimbletack?" Jared called softly.

He could never be sure when the house brownie was around.

Jared put the book down next to his latest project—a portrait of his dad. No one, not even Simon, knew that Jared had been practicing drawing. He wasn't very good—in fact, he was awful. But the Guide was for recording stuff, and to record well, he was going to have to learn to draw. Still, after today's humiliation, he didn't feel much like bothering. To be honest, he felt like tearing the picture of his father to pieces.

"There is a fell smell in the air," said a voice close to Jared's ear. "Best take care."

He whirled around to see a small nut-brown man dressed in a doll-size shirt and pants made from a dress sock. He was standing on one of the bookshelves at Jared's eye level, holding on to a piece of thread. At the top of the shelf, Jared could see the glint of a silver needle that the brownie had used to rappel down with.

"Thimbletack," Jared said, "what's wrong?"

"Could be trouble, could be nought. Whatever it is, it's what you wrought."

"What?"

"You kept the book despite my advice. Sooner or later there'll be a price."

"You always say that," said Jared. "What about the price for the sock you cut up to make your outfit? Don't tell me that was Aunt Lucinda's."

Thimbletack's eyes flashed. "Do not laugh, not today. You will learn to fear the fey."

Jared sighed and walked to the window. The last thing he needed was more trouble. Below, he could see the whole backyard. Mallory was close to the carriage house, stabbing at the air with her foil. Further out, near the broken-down plank fence that separated the yard from the nearby forest, Simon stood, hands cupped, probably calling for that stupid cat. Beyond that, thick trees obscured Jared's view. Downhill, in the distance, a highway cut through the woods, looking like a black snake in tall grass.

Thimbletack grabbed hold of the thread and swung over to the window ledge. He started to speak, then just stared outside. Finally he seemed to get his voice back. "Goblins in the wood. Doesn't look good. My warning comes too late. There's no help for your fate."

"Where?"

"By the fence. Have you no sense?"

Jared squinted and looked in the direction the brownie indicated. There was Simon, standing very still and staring at the grass in an odd way. Jared watched in horror as his brother started to struggle. Simon twisted and struck out, but there was nothing there.

"Simon!" Jared tried to force the window open, but it was nailed shut. He pounded on the glass.

Then Simon fell to the ground, still fighting some invisible foe. A moment later, he disappeared.

"I don't see anything!" he shouted at Thimbletack. "What is going on?"

Thimbletack's black eyes gleamed. "I had forgotten, your eyes are rotten. But there is a way, if you do what I say."

"You're talking about the Sight, aren't you?"

The brownie nodded.

"But how come I can see you and not the goblins?"

"We can choose to show what we want you to know."

Jared grabbed the Guide and ruffled through pages he knew nearly by heart: sketches, watercolor illustrations, and notes in his uncle's scratchy handwriting.

"Here," Jared said.

The little brownie leapt from the ledge to the desk.

The page beneath Jared's fingers showed different ways to get the Sight. He scanned quickly. "'Red hair. Being the seventh son of a seventh son. Faerie bathwater'?" He stopped at the last and looked up at Thimbletack, but the little brownie was pointing excitedly down the page. The illustration showed it clearly, a stone with a hole through the middle, like a ring.

"With the lens of stone, you can see what's

The little brownie was pointing excitedly.

not shown." With that, Thimbletack jumped from the desk. He skittered across the floor toward the door to the linen closet.

"We don't have time to look for rocks," Jared yelled, but what could he do except follow?

It smelled of gasoline and mildew.

Chapter Two

IN WHICH Several Things Are Taken, Including a Test

Thimbletack sprinted across the lawn, hopping from shadow to shadow. Mallory was still fencing against the wall of the old carriage house, her back to where Simon had been.

Jared walked up behind her and tugged the headphones off her ears by the cord.

She turned, foil pointing at his chest. "What?"

"Simon's been grabbed by goblins!"

Mallory's eyes narrowed. She looked around the lawn. "Goblins?"

"Must make haste." Thimbletack's voice was as shrill as a bird's. "No time to waste."

"Come on." Jared gestured toward the carriage house where the little brownie was waiting. "Before they get us."

"SIMON!" Mallory shouted.

"Shut up." Jared took her arm and yanked her into the carriage house, closing the door after them. "They're going to hear you."

"Who is going to hear me?" Mallory demanded. *"Goblins?"*

Jared ignored her.

Neither one of them had been inside the building before. It smelled of gasoline and mildew. A tarp covered an old black car. Shelves lined the walls, cluttered with metal tins and mason jars half-filled with brown and yellow liquids. There were even stalls where horses must have been stabled long ago. A stack of boxes and leather trunks occupied one corner.

Thimbletack hopped up on a can of paint and pointed toward the boxes. "Hurry! Hurry! If they come, we must scurry!"

"If Simon got grabbed by goblins, why are we rooting through garbage?" Mallory asked.

"Here," Jared said, holding out the book and pointing to the picture of the stone. "We're looking for *this*."

"Oh, great," she said. "It'll be so easy to find in this mess."

"Just hurry," said Jared.

The first trunk contained a saddle, a few bridles, some combs, and other equipment for taking care of horses. Simon would have been fascinated. Jared and Mallory opened the next box together. It was full of old, rusted tools. Then they found a few boxes stuffed with tableware wrapped in dirty towels.

"Aunt Lucinda must have never thrown out anything," Jared said.

"Here's another one." Mallory sighed as she dragged a small wooden crate over to her brother. The top slid open in a dusty groove, revealing wadded up newspapers.

"Look how old these are," Mallory said. "This one says 1910."

"I didn't even think there were newspapers in 1910," said Jared.

Inside each crumpled piece of paper was a different item. Jared unrolled one to discover a pair of metal binoculars. In another he found a magnifying glass. The print below it was made huge. "This one's from 1927. They're all different."

Jared picked up another page. "'Girl drowns in empty well.' Weird."

"Hey, look at this." Mallory straightened one of the sheets. "1885. 'Local boy lost.' Says he was eaten by a bear. Look at the surviving brother's name! 'Arthur Spiderwick.'"

"There it is! This is his!" Thimbletack said, climbing into the box. When he resurfaced, he held the strangest eyepiece Jared had ever seen.

It covered only a single eye and attached to

The strangest eyepiece

the face with an adjustable nose clip as well as two leather straps and a chain. Backed in stiff, brown leather, four metal clamps waited to hold a lens of some kind. But the strangest thing about the device was the series of magnifying lenses on movable metal arms.

Thimbletack let Jared take the eyepiece and turn it over in his hands. Then he took a smooth stone with a hole through the center from behind his back.

"The lens of stone." Jared reached for it.

Thimbletack stepped back. "Here you must prove yourself or get nothing from this elf."

Jared stared in horror. "We don't have time for games."

"Time or not, you must tell if you will use this stone well."

"I only need it to find Simon," Jared said. "I'll give it right back."

Thimbletack cocked an eyebrow.

Jared tried again. "I promise that I won't let anyone use it—except Mallory—and, well, Simon. Come on! You're the one that suggested the stone in the first place."

"A human boy is like a snake. His promises are easy to break."

Jared's eyes narrowed. He could feel the frustration and anger rising up in him. His hands curled into fists. "Give me the stone."

Thimbletack said nothing.

"Give it to me."

"Jared?" Mallory cautioned.

But Jared barely heard her. There was a roaring in his ears as he reached out and grabbed hold of Thimbletack. The little brownie squirmed in his grasp, abruptly changing shape into a lizard, a rat that bit Jared's hand, then a slippery eel that flailed wetly. Jared was bigger, though, and he held fast. Finally, the stone dropped free, hitting the floor with a clatter. Jared covered it with his foot before he let

Thimbletack go. The brownie disappeared as Jared picked up the stone.

"Maybe you shouldn't have done that," said Mallory.

"I don't care." Jared put his bitten finger in his mouth. "We have to find Simon."

"Does that thing work?" Mallory asked.

"Let's see." Jared held the stone up to his eye and looked out the window.

"They're headed right for us."

Chapter Three

IN WHICH Mallory Finally Gets to Put Her Rapier to Good Use

Through the small hole in the stone, Jared saw goblins. There were five of them, all with faces like frogs' and eyes that were dead white with no pupil at all. Hairless, cat-like ears stuck up from their heads, and their teeth were pieces of shattered glass and small, jagged rocks. Their green, bloated bodies moved swiftly over the lawn. One held a stained sack while the rest scented the air like dogs, moving in the direction of the carriage house. Jared backed away from the window, almost tripping on an old bucket.

"They're headed right for us," he whispered, ducking down.

Mallory gripped her foil more tightly, knuckles white. "What about Simon?"

"I didn't see him."

She lifted up her head and peered outside. "I don't see *anything,*" she said.

Jared crouched down with the stone clutched in his palm. He could hear the goblins outside, grunting and shuffling as they got closer. He didn't dare look through the stone again.

Then Jared heard the sound of old wood snapping.

A rock hit one of the windows.

"They're coming," Jared said. He shoved the Guide into his backpack, not bothering to buckle it.

"Coming?" Mallory replied. "I think they're here."

Claws scraped at the side of the barn and little barks came from beneath the window. Jared's stomach turned to lead. He couldn't move.

"We have to do something," he whispered.

"We're going to have to make a run for the house," Mallory whispered back.

"We can't," Jared said. The memory of the goblins' jagged teeth and claws wouldn't leave him.

"A couple more planks and they'll be inside."

He nodded numbly, steeling himself to rise. Fumbling, he tried to fit the stone into the eyepiece and attach it to his head. The clip pinched his nose.

"On my mark," said Mallory. "One. Two. Three. Go!"

She opened the door and they both sprinted toward the house. Goblins hurtled after them. Clawed hands caught at Jared's clothes. He wrenched free and ran on.

Mallory was faster. She was almost to the door of the house when a goblin caught the back of Jared's shirt and pulled hard. He went down on his stomach in the grass. The stone flew out of the monocle. He dug his fingers into the dirt, holding on as much as he could, but he was being dragged backward.

He could feel the clasps on his pack loosening, and he screamed.

Mallory turned. Instead of running on toward the house, she started running back to him. Her fencing sword was still in her hand, but there was no way she could know what she was up against.

He was being dragged backward.

"Mallory!" Jared shouted. "No! Run away!"

At least one goblin must have gone past him, because he saw Mallory's arm jerk and heard her cry out. Red lines appeared where nails scraped her. The headphones were ripped free from her neck. She spun and lashed out with the rapier, dealing a stinging blow to the air. It didn't seem like she had hit anything. She swung the sword in an arc, but again, nothing.

Jared kicked out hard with one of his legs, striking something solid. He felt the grip that held him slip, and he pulled himself forward, yanking his backpack out of their grasp. The contents spilled out and Jared was barely able to snatch up the Guide in time. Reaching around in the grass, he picked up the stone and scrambled to where Mallory was. Then he brought the stone to his eye and looked.

"Six o'clock," he shouted, and Mallory whirled, striking in that direction, catching a goblin across the ear. It howled. Rapier blades didn't have points but they sure stung when they hit.

"Shorter, they're shorter." Jared managed to pull himself to his feet so that he was standing with his back against Mallory's. All five goblins were circling them.

One lunged from the right. "Three o'clock," Jared shouted.

Mallory knocked the goblin to the ground easily.

"Twelve o'clock! Nine o'clock! Seven o'clock!" They were rushing all at once, and Jared didn't think Mallory could possibly manage. He hefted the field guide and swung it as hard as he could at the nearest goblin.

Thwack! The book hit the goblin hard enough to send it sprawling backward.

All five goblins were circling them.

Mallory had knocked down two more with hard blows. Now they circled more warily, gnashing teeth of glass and stone.

There was a strange call, like a cross between a bark and a whistle.

At that sound, the goblins retreated one by one into the woods.

Jared collapsed onto the grass. His side hurt and he was out of breath.

"They're gone," Jared said. He held out the stone to Mallory. "Look."

Mallory sat down next to him and held it up to her eye. "I don't see anything, but I didn't see anything a minute ago either."

"They still might come back." Jared rolled over and opened the Guide, flipping through the pages quickly. "Read this."

"'Goblins travel in roving bands looking for trouble.'" Mallory scowled at the words. "And look, Jared—'Cats and dogs missing is a sign that goblins are in the area.'"

They exchanged a glance. "Tibbs," Jared said with a shudder.

Mallory read on. "'Goblins are born without teeth and so find substitutes, such as the fangs of animals, sharp rocks, and pieces of glass.'"

"But it doesn't say anything about how to stop them," said Jared. "Or where they might have taken Simon."

Mallory didn't look up from the page.

Jared tried to keep his mind from imagining what the goblins might want with Simon. It seemed pretty obvious to him what they did with the cats and dogs, but he didn't want to believe that his brother could be . . . could be *eaten*. His gaze fell on the illustration of those horrible teeth.

Surely not. Surely there was some other explanation.

Mallory took a deep breath and pointed to the illustration. "It's going to be dark soon, and with eyes like that, they probably have better night vision than we do."

That was pretty smart. Jared resolved to write a note in the Guide about it when they got Simon back. He took off the eyepiece and slid the stone into place again, but the clamps were too loose to hold it.

"It doesn't work," Jared said.

"You have to adjust it," said Mallory. "We need a screwdriver or something."

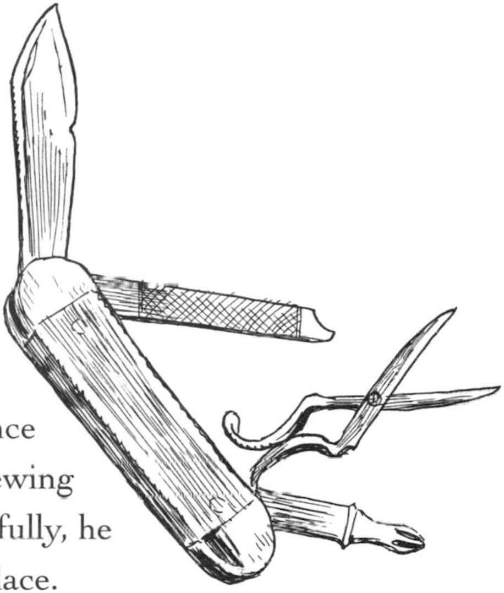

Jared took a pocketknife from the back pocket of his pants. It had a screwdriver, a little knife, a magnifying glass, a file, bent scissors, and a place where there had once been a toothpick. Screwing down the clamps carefully, he fitted the stone into place.

"Here, let me tie it on your head right." Mallory knotted the leather straps until the monocle-apparatus was on tight. Jared had to squint a little to see properly, but it was much better than before.

"Take this," Mallory said, and handed him a practice rapier. The end wasn't pointed,

Time to find Simon

though, so he wasn't sure how much real damage it could do.

Still, it felt better to be armed. Tucking the Guide into his backpack, tightening the straps, and holding the sword in front of him, Jared started back down the hill into the darkening woods.

It was time to find Simon.

The air was different.

Chapter Four

IN WHICH Jared and Mallory Find Many Things, but Not What They're Looking For

Stepping into the woods, Jared felt a slight chill. The air was different, full of the smell of green things and fresh dirt, but the light was murky. He and Mallory stepped through tangles of jewelweed and past thin trees heaped with vines. Somewhere above them a bird started calling, making a harsh sound like an alarm. Beneath their footsteps, the ground was slick with moss. Twigs snapped as they passed and Jared heard the distant sound of water.

There was a streak of brown, and a small owl settled on a low branch. Its head cocked toward them as it bit into the small, limp mouse in its claw.

Mallory pushed through a knot of bushes, and Jared followed. Tiny burrs caught on his clothes and in his hair. They sidled around the crumbling trunk of a fallen tree swarming with black ants.

There was something different about his vision with the stone in place. Everything was brighter and more clear. But there was something else, too. Things moved in the grass, in the trees, things he couldn't quite see but was aware of for the first time. Faces made of bark and rock and moss that he only saw for an instant. It was as though the whole of the forest was alive.

"There." Mallory fingered a broken branch

and pointed to where clumps of ferns had been trampled. "That's the way they went."

They followed the trail of smashed weeds and snapped branches until they came to a stream. By then the woods had grown more shadowed, and the twilight sounds had increased. A cloud of gnats settled on them for a moment, then blew out toward the water.

"What do we do now?" Mallory asked. "Can you see anything?"

Jared squinted through the eyepiece and shook his head. "Let's just follow the stream. The trail has to pick up again."

They walked on through the forest.

"Mallory," Jared whispered, pointing at a huge oak tree. Tiny green and brown creatures were perched on a branch. Their wings resembled leaves, but their faces seemed almost human. Instead of hair, grass and flower buds grew from their tiny heads.

"What are you looking at?" Mallory raised her rapier and took two steps backward.

Jared shook his head slightly. "Sprites . . . I think."

"Why do you have that stupid expression on your face?"

"They're just . . ." He couldn't quite explain. He extended his hand, palm up, and stared in amazement as one of the creatures alighted on his finger. Soft feet tickled his skin as the tiny faerie blinked up at him with black eyes.

"Jared," Mallory said impatiently.

At the sound of her voice, the sprite jumped into the air. Jared watched as it spiraled upward into the leaves above.

The patches of sunlight filtering through the trees became tinged with orange. Up ahead

the stream widened where it ran under the remains of a stone bridge.

Jared could feel his skin prickle as they got closer to the rubble, but there was no sign of goblins. The stream was very wide, almost

One alighted on his finger.

ENSION HOOK-AND-LADDER TRUCK.

ie Fire Department.

istory of Its Growth from a Volunteer Bucket Brigade to a Paid System.

Ample for Every Emergency—Names of Its Past Chiefs and Present Membership.

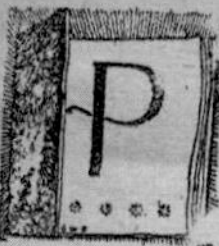

RIOR to 1826 the citizens of Erie had no protection against fire. In Februrary of that year "Active" Fire company was organized. Nearly all the able-bodied men in the place were enrolled as members, and R. S. Reed was the first chief engineer. Buckets were used at first. In 1830 a small hand fire engine was purchased from the Pittsburg fire department and used for several years In 1837 a rival company, called the "Red Jackets," was formed. In 1839 two companies, the "Perry" and the "Eagle," were organized. In 1844 the "Mechanics" made their first appearance at a fire. In 1848 the "Vulcan" was formed. The "Phœnix" hook and ladder company came out in 1852. The Parade Street Company was formed in 1861.

The first city fire organization with general officers was formed in 1851, but was not very effective until 10 years later, when a third-class Amoskeag steamer was purchased. As the population increased and disastrous fires became more numerous, the people became clamorous for a more efficient fire organization, which was finally affected.

Erie now has one of the best organized, best disciplined and most efficient fire depart-

Continued on page 19.

THEODORE SPIDERWICK, Age 10

Local Boy Lost

Authorities Confirm Lost Lad Was Another Victim of Bear Attack

THE Springfield police department has confirmed that ten-year-old Theodore Spiderwick, missing since early last Thurday evening, is yet another victim of the bear attacks that have now claimed the lives of at least three other children.

The boy's younger brother, Arthur, age 8, was witness to the heinous attack and claimed the bear "was at least seven feet tall, with huge fangs and looked like a troll."

When asked to comment on the young boy's statement, officer K. L. Lewis mentioned that "the lad seemed to be severely affected and distressed" and that his "imagination must be running wild with all of the confusion and speculation surrounding his older brother Theodore's disappearance."

Officer Lewis also commented that the community should be asked to "keep a watchful

Continued on page 19.

Clipping from Pennsylvania newspaper reporting the "disappearance" of Arthur Spiderwick's older brother, Theodore, in 1885. Found among Arthur Spiderwick's papers

twenty feet across, and there was a darkness in the middle that seemed to speak of deep water.

Jared heard a distant sound like metal grating against metal.

Mallory stopped, looked across the water, and raised her head. "Did you hear that?"

"Could it be Simon?" Jared asked. He hoped it wasn't. It didn't sound human at all.

"I don't know," Mallory said, "but whatever it was, it's got something to do with those goblins. Come on!" With that, Mallory bounded in the direction of the noise.

"Don't go in there, Mallory," Jared said. "It's too deep."

"Don't be a baby," she said, and waded into the stream. She made two long strides and then dropped as though she had stepped off the edge of a cliff. Dark green water closed over her head.

Jared lunged forward. Dropping his rapier onto the bank, he plunged his hand into icy cold water. His sister bobbed to the surface, sputtering. She grabbed for his arm.

He had pulled her halfway onto the bank when something began to surface behind her. At first it seemed like a hill rising from the water, stony and covered in moss. Then a head emerged, the deep green of rotten river grass, with small black eyes, a nose that was gnarled like a branch, and a mouth full of cracked teeth. A hand reached toward them. Its fingers were as long as roots, and its nails were black with murk. Jared breathed in the stench of the bottom of the pool, putrid leaves, and old, old mud.

He screamed. His mind went completely blank. He couldn't move.

Mallory pulled herself the rest of the way onto the bank and looked over her shoulder.

Something began to surface.

"What is it? What do you see?"

At her voice, Jared snapped into moving and stumbled woodenly away from the stream, tugging her along with him. "Troll," he gasped.

The creature lunged after them. Long fingers dragged through the grass just short of where they were. Then the creature howled and Jared looked back, but he couldn't see what had happened. It felt toward them again but jerked away when one long finger fell into a beam of light. The monster bellowed.

"The sun," Jared said. "It got burned by the sun."

"There's not much sun left," Mallory replied. "Let's go."

"Waaait," the monster whispered. Its voice was soft.

Yellow eyes regarded them steadily. "Cooome baaack. I haaave something for youuu." The troll extended a closed hand as though something might indeed be clutched in its palm.

"Jared, come on." Mallory's voice was almost pleading. "I can't see what you're talking to."

"Have you seen my brother?" Jared asked.

"Perhaaaps. I heard something a tiiime ago, but it was bright, too bright to look."

"That was him! It must have been. Where did they go?"

The head swung toward the remnants of the

bridge and then looked back at Jared. "Cooome closer and I will tell you."

Jared took a step back. "No way."

"Aaat leassst cooome geeet youuur sss-word." The troll gestured to the rapier beside itself. The sword was lying on the bank, where Jared had dropped it. He looked over at his sister. Her hands were empty too. She must have left her sword at the bottom of the pool.

Mallory took a half-step forward. "That's the only weapon we have."

"Cooome and taaake it. I will clooose my eyeees if it will maake you feeel saaafer." One huge hand covered its eyes.

Mallory looked at the sword in the mud. Her eyes focused on it in a way that made Jared very nervous. She was thinking about trying for it.

"You can't even see the thing," Jared hissed. "Let's go."

"But the sword . . ."

Jared untied the eyepiece and held it out to her. Her face went pale at the sight of the massive creature, peeking through a gap in its fingers, imprisoned only by the fading patches of sunlight.

"Come on," she said shakily.

"Noooo," called the troll. "Cooome baaack. I'll eeeven tuuurn arooound. I'll cooount to ten. It'll beee a faaair chaaance. Come baaaack."

Jared and Mallory ran on through the woods until they found a patch of sunlight to stop in.

Both leaned against the thick trunk of an oak and tried to catch their breath. Mallory was shivering. Jared didn't know if it was because she was soaked or because of the troll. He unzipped his sweatshirt, took it off, and handed it to her.

"We're lost," Mallory said between gulps of air. "And we're unarmed."

"At least we know they couldn't have crossed the stream," said Jared, struggling to tie the eyepiece back on his head. "The troll would have gotten them for sure."

"But the sound was on the other side." Mallory kicked a tree, chipping off bark.

Jared's nose caught the scent of something burning. It was faint, but he thought it smelled like scorched hair.

"Do you smell that?" Jared asked.

"That way," Mallory said.

They crashed through the brush, heedless of the scratches twigs and thorns made along their arms. Jared's thoughts were all of his brother and fire.

"Look at this." Mallory stopped abruptly. She reached into the grass and picked up a single brown shoe.

"It's Simon's."

"I know," Mallory said. She turned it over, but Jared couldn't see any clues, except that it was muddy.

"You don't think he's . . ." Jared couldn't bring himself to say it.

"No, I don't!" Mallory shoved the shoe in the front pocket of her sweatshirt.

He nodded slowly, allowing himself to be convinced.

A little farther, and the trees began to thin. They stepped out onto a highway. Black

A single brown shoe

asphalt stretched off into the distant horizon. Behind it all, the sun was setting in a blaze of purple and orange.

And on the shoulder of the road, in the distance, a group of goblins huddled around a fire.

Sinister wind chimes

Chapter Five

IN WHICH the Fate of the Missing Cat Is Discovered

Jared and Mallory approached the goblin camp cautiously, dodging from trunk to trunk. Broken bits of glass and gnawed bones littered the ground. High in the trees they could see cages woven from thornbushes, plastic bags, and other refuse. Squashed soda cans hung from the branches, clattering together like sinister wind chimes.

Ten goblins sat around a fire. The blackened body of something that looked a lot like a cat turned on a stick. Every now and then one

"Skin it raw, skin the fat."

of the goblins would lean over to lick the charred meat, and the goblin turning the spit would bark loudly. Then they would all start barking.

Several of the goblins started to sing. Jared shuddered at the words.

Fidirol, Fidirat!
Catch a dog, catch a cat
Skin it raw, skin the fat
On the spit, turn like that
Fidirol, Fidirat!

Cars whizzed by, oblivious. Perhaps even their mother was driving past now, Jared thought.

"How many?" Mallory whispered, hefting a heavy branch.

"Ten," Jared answered. "I don't see Simon. He must be in one of those cages."

"Are you sure?" Mallory squinted in the direction of the goblins. "Give me that thing."

"Not now," said Jared.

They moved slowly through the trees looking for a cage large enough to contain Simon. Ahead of them, something cried out, shrill and loud. They crept forward to the edge of the forest.

An animal was lying alongside the road, beyond the goblin camp. It was the size of a car, but curled up, with a hawk's head and the body of a lion. Its flank was streaked with blood.

"What do you see?"

"A griffin," said Jared. "It's hurt."

"What's a griffin?"

"It's kind of a bird, kind of a—never mind, just stay away from it."

Mallory sighed, moving deeper into the woods.

"There," she said. "What about those?"

Jared looked up. Several of the high cages were larger, and he thought he could make out a human shape in one of them. Simon!

"I can climb up," Jared said.

Mallory nodded. "Be fast."

Jared wedged his foot in a hollow of the bark, hefting himself up to the first split in the branches. Then, pulling himself higher, he started crawling along the bough that held the little cages. If he stood up on that limb, he would be looking into the cages that were hung higher.

As he edged along, Jared could not help looking down. In the cages below, he could see squirrels, cats, and birds. Some were clawing and biting at the bars, while others were unmoving. A few contained just bones. They were all lined with leaves that looked suspiciously like poison ivy.

"Hey, dribble-puss, over here."

The voice surprised Jared so much he almost lost his grip on the branch. It had come from one of the large cages.

"Who's there?" Jared whispered.

"Hogsqueal. Now how about opening that door?"

Jared saw the frog face of another goblin, but this one had green cat's eyes. It was wearing clothes, and its teeth weren't glass or metal, but what looked like *baby* teeth.

"I don't think so," said Jared. "You can rot in there. I'm not letting you out."

"Don't be a cat-whipper, beetlehead. If I holler, those guys are going to make you into dessert."

"I bet you yell all the time," Jared said. "I bet they don't believe anything you say."

"HEY! LOOK–"

Jared grabbed the edge of the cage and pulled it forward. Hogsqueal went quiet. Below, the goblins slapped one other and snatched pieces of cat meat, apparently unaware of the racket in the tree.

"Okay, okay," Jared said.

"Good. Let me out!" the goblin demanded.

"I have to find my brother. Tell me where he is, and then I'll let you out."

"No way, candy butt. You must think I'm as dumb as a hatful of worms. You let me out or I scream again."

"Jared!" Simon's voice called from one of the cages farther down the branch. "I'm over here."

"I'm coming," Jared called back, turning toward the sound.

"You open this door or I scream," the goblin threatened.

Jared took a deep breath. "You won't scream. If you scream, they'll catch me and then no one's going to let you out. I'm getting my brother out first, but I'll be back for you."

Jared edged farther down the branch. He was relieved that the goblin stayed silent.

Simon was stuffed in a cage much too small for him. His legs were drawn up against his chest, and the toes of one foot stuck through the bars. His bare skin was scraped from the thorns that lined the cage.

"You okay?" Jared asked, taking his pocketknife out and sawing at the knotted

"You okay?"

vines wrapped around Simon's prison.

"I'm fine." Simon's voice quavered just a little.

Jared wanted to ask if Simon had found Tibbs, but he was afraid of the answer. "I'm sorry," he said finally. "I should have helped look for the cat."

"That's okay," said Simon, squeezing out through the part of the door Jared managed to open. "But I have to tell you that—"

"Turtle-head! Boy! Enough mouth! Let me out!" the goblin shouted.

"Come on," said Jared. "I said I'd help him."

Simon followed his twin back along the branch to Hogsqueal's cage.

"What's in there?"

"A goblin, I think."

"A goblin!" Simon exclaimed. "Are you crazy?"

"I can spit in your eye," Hogsqueal offered.

"Gross," said Simon. "No, thanks."

"It will give you the Sight, jinglebrains. Here," Hogsqueal said, taking a handkerchief from one of his pockets and spitting in it. "Rub this on your eyes."

Jared hesitated. Could he trust a goblin? But then, Hogsqueal would be stuck in the cage forever if he did anything bad. Simon would never let the goblin out.

He took off the eyepiece and wiped the dirty cloth over his eyes. It made them sting.

"Ugh. That's the most disgusting thing ever," said Simon.

Jared blinked and looked over at the goblins sitting around their fire. He could see them without the stone. "Simon, it works!"

Simon looked at the cloth skeptically but rubbed his own eyes with goblin spit.

"We had a deal, right? Let me out," Hogsqueal demanded.

"Tell me what you're in there for, first," said Jared. Giving them the handkerchief was nice, but it could still be a trick.

"You're not very chicken-beaked for a nib-head," the goblin grumbled. "I'm in here for letting out one of the cats. See, I like cats, and not just 'cause they're tasty, which they are, no mistake. But they got these eyes that are an awful lot like mine, and this one was real little, not much meat there. And she had this sweet little mewl." The goblin looked lost in his memory, then abruptly looked back at Jared. "So enough about that. Let me out."

"And what about your teeth? Do you eat babies or what?" Jared had not found the goblin's story very reassuring.

"What is this? An interrogation?" Hogsqueal groused.

"I'm letting you out already." Jared came closer and started to cut the complicated knots on the cage. "But I want to know about your teeth."

"Well, kids got this quaint idea of leaving teeth under their pillows, see?"

"You steal kids' teeth?"

"Come on, Dumbellina, tell me you don't believe in the tooth fairy!"

Jared fumbled for a few more moments, saying nothing. He had the last knot almost sawed through when the griffin started screeching.

Four of the goblins circled it with pointed sticks. The animal couldn't seem to raise itself very far off the ground, but it could snap at the goblins if they got too close. Then the creature's hawk beak connected, scissoring off a goblin arm. The wounded goblin squealed while a second drove his stick into the griffin's back. The remaining goblins cheered.

"What are they doing?" Jared whispered.

"What does it look like?" Hogsqueal replied. "They're waiting for it to die."

"They're killing him!" Simon yelled. His eyes were wide, staring down at the gruesome spectacle. Jared realized that his brother was seeing all this for the first time. Suddenly Simon grabbed a handful of leaves and sticks from the tree they were standing on and hurled them at the goblins below.

"Simon, stop it!" Jared said.

"Leave him alone, you jerks!" Simon shouted. "LEAVE HIM ALONE!"

All of the goblins looked up at that moment, their eyes reflecting a ghostly pale white in the dark.

The flames blazed green.

Chapter Six

IN WHICH Jared Is Forced to Make a Difficult Choice

"Let me OUT!" Hogsqueal yelled. Jared snapped into motion and cut through the last knot.

Hogsqueal danced onto the branch, heedless of the goblins barking beneath him. They had begun to surround the tree.

Jared looked around for some kind of weapon, but all he had was his little knife. Simon was breaking off more branches and Hogsqueal was running away, jumping from tree to tree like a monkey. He and his brother were abandoned and trapped. If they tried to climb down, the goblins would be upon them.

And somewhere down there, in the gloom, Mallory was alone and blind. Her only protection was the red of the sweatshirt she wore.

"What about the animals in the cages?" Simon asked.

"No time!"

"Hey, mucky-pups!" Jared heard Hogsqueal shout. He looked in the direction of the voice, but Hogsqueal wasn't talking to them at all. He was dancing around the campfire and sticking a large strip of burnt cat meat in his mouth.

"Ninnyhammers!" he yelled at the other goblins. "Pestleheads! Goobernuts! Jibbernolls! Fiddlewizzits!" He leaned back and urinated on the fire, making the flames blaze green.

The goblins turned from the tree and headed right for Hogsqueal.

"Move!" Jared said. "Now!"

Simon climbed down the tree as fast as he could, jumping once he was close enough. He fell to the ground with a soft thud. Jared landed beside him.

Mallory hugged them both, but she didn't let go of her stick.

"I heard the goblins get close, but I couldn't see a thing," she said.

"Put this on." Jared held out the eyepiece to her.

"You need it," she protested.

"Now!" Jared said.

Surprisingly Mallory buckled it on without another word. After it was on, she reached into her sweatshirt and gave Simon his shoe.

They started moving into the woods, but Jared couldn't help looking back. Hogsqueal was surrounded like the griffin had been only moments before.

They couldn't leave him like that.

"Hey!" he called. "Over here!"

The goblins turned and, seeing the three children, started moving toward them.

Jared, Mallory, and Simon started to run.

"Are you crazy?" Mallory yelled.

"He was helping us," Jared yelled back. He couldn't be sure she'd heard him since he was panting at the same time he was speaking.

"Where are we going?" Simon shouted.

"The stream," said Jared. He was thinking fast, faster than he'd ever thought in his life. The troll was their only chance. He was sure that it could stop ten goblins with no problem. What he wasn't sure of was how they could avoid it themselves.

"We can't go this way," Mallory said. Jared ignored her.

If only they could jump the stream, maybe

that would be enough. The goblins wouldn't know there was a monster to avoid.

The goblins were still far enough behind. They wouldn't see what was coming.

Almost there. Jared could see the stream ahead, but they weren't to the ruined bridge yet.

Then Jared saw something that stopped him cold. The troll was out of the water. It stood at the edge of the bank, eyes and teeth gleaming in the moonlight. Even hunched over, Jared guessed that it was more than ten feet tall.

"Luckyyyy meee," it said, reaching out a long arm in their direction.

"Wait," said Jared.

The creature moved toward them, a slow smile showing broken teeth. It definitely was not waiting.

"Hear that?" Jared asked. "That's goblins.

It stood at the edge of the bank.

Ten fat goblins. That's a lot more than three skinny kids."

The monster hesitated. The Guide had said that trolls weren't very smart. Jared hoped that was true.

"All you have to do is get back in the stream and we'll lead them right to you. I promise."

The yellow eyes of the creature glinted greedily. "Yesss," it said.

"Hurry!" Jared said. "They're almost here!"

It slid toward the water and dropped under with barely a ripple.

"What was that?" Simon asked.

Jared was shaking, but he could not let that stop him. "Go in the stream there, where it's shallow. We have to get them to chase us through the water."

"Are you nuts?" Mallory demanded.

"Please," Jared begged. "Trust me."

"We have to do something!" said Simon.

"Okay, let's go." Mallory followed her brothers toward the muddy bank, shaking her head.

The goblins burst through the trees. Jared, Mallory, and Simon waded through the shallow water, zigzagging around the pit. The fastest way to go after them would be to cut through the middle of the stream.

Jared heard the goblins splashing behind them, barking madly. Then the barks turned to squeals. Jared looked back to see a few goblins paddling for the shore. The troll grabbed them

all, shaking and biting and dragging them down to his watery lair.

Jared tried not to look any more. His stomach did an odd, nauseous flip-flop.

Simon looked pale and a little queasy.

"Let's go home," Mallory said.

Jared nodded.

"We can't," said Simon. "What about all those animals?"

The full moon overhead

Chapter Seven

IN WHICH Simon Outdoes Himself and Finds an Extraordinary New Pet

"You have to be kidding," Mallory said when Simon explained what he wanted to do.

"They're going to die if we don't," Simon insisted. "The griffin is bleeding."

"The griffin, too?" Jared asked. He understood about the cats, but a griffin?

"How are we going to help that thing?" Mallory demanded. "We're not faerie veterinarians!"

"We have to try," said Simon just as firmly.

Jared owed it to Simon to agree. After all, he had put Simon through a lot. "We could get the old tarp from the carriage house."

"Yeah," Simon chimed in. "Then we could drag the griffin back to the house. There's plenty of room."

Mallory rolled her eyes.

"If it lets us," Jared said. "Did you see what it did to that goblin?"

"Come on, guys," Simon pleaded. "I'm not strong enough to pull it alone."

"All right," she said. "But I'm not standing close to the head."

Jared, Simon, and Mallory trooped back to the carriage house. The full moon overhead gave them enough light to navigate the woods, but they were still careful, crossing the stream where it was barely a trickle. At the edge of the lawn, Jared could see that the windows of the main house were lit and that his mother's car was parked in the gravel driveway. Was she making dinner? Had she called the police? Jared wanted to go inside and tell his mom that they were all okay, but he didn't dare.

"Jared, come on." Simon had opened the door to the carriage house, and Mallory was pulling the tarp from the old car.

"Hey, look at this." Simon picked up a flashlight from one of the shelves and flicked it on. Luckily, no beam of light spread across the lawn.

"Batteries are probably dead," Jared said.

"Stop playing around," Mallory told them. "We're trying *not* to get caught."

They dragged the tarp back through the woods. The walk went more slowly and with a good deal of arguing about the shortest way. Jared couldn't keep from jumping at distant

night noises. Even the croaking of frogs sounded ominous. He couldn't help wondering what else there was, hidden in the dark. Maybe something worse than goblins or trolls. He shook his head and reminded himself that no one could possibly be that unlucky in one day.

When they finally found the goblin camp again, Jared was surprised to see Hogsqueal sitting by the fire. He was licking bones and burped contentedly when they approached.

"I guess you're okay," Jared said.

"Is that any way to talk to someone who saved your prawnheaded hide?"

Jared started to protest—they'd almost gotten killed over the stupid goblin—but Mallory grabbed his arm.

"Help Simon with the animals," she said. "I'll watch the goblin."

"I'm not a goblin," Hogsqueal said. "I'm a *hob*goblin."

"Whatever," said Mallory, sitting on a rock.

Simon and Jared climbed the trees, letting out all the animals in the cages. Most ran down the nearest branch or sprang for the ground, as afraid of the boys as they were of the goblins. One little kitten crouched in the back of a cage, mewling pitifully. Jared didn't know what to do with it, so he put it in his backpack and kept moving. There was no sign of Tibbs.

When Simon saw the kitten, he insisted that they keep it. Jared wished that he meant instead of the griffin.

Jared thought that Hogsqueal's eyes softened when he saw

the cat, but that might have been from hunger.

When the cages were empty, the three siblings and the hobgoblin approached the griffin. It watched them warily, extending its claws.

Mallory dropped her end of the tarp. "You know, hurt animals sometimes just attack."

"Sometimes they don't, though," said Simon, walking toward the griffin with open hands. "Sometimes they just let you take care of them. I found a rat like that once. It only bit me when it got better."

"Only a bunch of chuckleheads would mess with a wounded griffin." Hogsqueal cracked open another bone and started sucking out the marrow. "You want me to hold that kitten?"

Mallory scowled at him. "You want to follow your friends to the bottom of the stream?"

Jared smiled. It was good to have Mallory on their side.

That made him think of something. "Since you're feeling so generous, how about a little goblin spit for my sister?"

"It's *hob*goblin spit," Hogsqueal said loftily.

"Gee, thanks," Mallory said, "but I'll pass."

"No, look—it gives you the Sight. And that even makes sense," Jared said. "I mean, if faerie bathwater works, then this should too."

"I can't even begin to express how disgusting those choices are."

"Well, if that's how she feels about it." Hogsqueal was apparently trying to look offended. Jared didn't think he was succeeding at it too well, because he was licking a bone at the same time.

"Mal, come on. You can't wear a stone strapped to your head all the time."

"Says you," she replied. "Do you even know how long this spit is going to last?"

Jared hadn't really considered that. He looked at Hogsqueal.

"Until someone pokes out your eyes," the faerie said.

"Well, then great," Jared said, trying to get back some control of the conversation.

Mallory sighed. "Fine, fine." She knelt

"I'm not going to hurt you."

down and removed the monocle. Hogsqeal spit with great relish.

Looking up, Jared noticed that Simon had already gone over to the griffin. He was squatting down beside it and whispering.

"Hello, griffin," Simon was saying in his most soothing voice. "I'm not going to hurt you. We're just going to help you get better. Come on, be good."

The griffin let out a whine like a kettle's whistle. Simon stroked its feathers lightly.

"Go ahead and spread out the tarp," Simon whispered.

The griffin raised itself slightly, opening its beak, but Simon's petting seemed to relax it. It put its head back down on the asphalt.

They unrolled the tarp behind it.

Simon knelt down by its head, talking softly with cooing words. The griffin appeared to be listening, ruffling its feathers as though Simon's whispers might tickle.

Mallory crept up to one side of it and gently took hold of its front paws, and Jared took hold of the back.

"One, two, three," they said together softly, then rolled the griffin onto the tarp. It squawked and flailed its legs, but by that time it was on the canvas.

Then they lifted it as much as they could and began the arduous process of dragging the griffin to the carriage house. It was lighter than Jared expected. Simon suggested that it might have hollow bones like a bird.

"So long, chidderblains," Hogsqueal called after them.

"See you around," Jared called back. He almost wished the hobgoblin was coming with them.

Mallory rolled her eyes.

The griffin did not enjoy its trip. They couldn't lift it up too far, so it got dragged over bumps and bushes a lot. It screeched and squawked and fluttered its good wing. They had to stop and wait for Simon to calm it down and then start dragging again. It seemed to take forever to get the griffin back home.

Once at the carriage house, they had to open the double doors in the back and haul the griffin into one of the horse stalls. It settled in some of the old straw.

Simon knelt down to clean the griffin's wounds as well as he could by moonlight and with only water from the hose. Jared got a bucket and filled it for the griffin to drink. It gulped gratefully.

Even Mallory pitched in, finding a moth-

At the carriage house

eaten blanket to drape over the animal. It almost looked tame, bandaged and sleepy in the carriage house.

Even though Jared thought it was crazy to bring the griffin back there, he had to admit that he was starting to have a little affection for it. More than he had for Hogsqueal, at any rate.

By the time Jared, Simon, and Mallory limped into the house, it was very late. Mallory was still damp from her fall into the stream, and Simon's clothes were scratched nearly to tatters. Jared had grass stains on his pants and scraped elbows from his chase through the woods. But they still had the book and the eyepiece, and Simon was carrying a kitten the color of butterscotch toffee, and all of them were still alive. From where Jared stood, those things counted as huge successes.

Their mother was on the phone when they came in. Her face was blotchy with tears.

"They're here!" She hung up the phone and stared at them for a moment. "Where were you? It is one o'clock in the morning!" She pointed her finger at Mallory. "How could you be so irresponsible?"

Mallory looked over at Jared. Simon, on his other side, looked at him too and clutched the cat to his chest. It suddenly occurred to Jared that they were waiting for him to come up with an excuse.

"Um . . . there was a cat in a tree," Jared started. Simon gave him an encouraging smile. "That cat." Jared indicated the kitten in Simon's arms. "And, you see, Simon climbed up the tree, but the kitten got scared. It climbed up even farther and Simon got stuck. And I ran back and got Mallory."

"And I tried to climb after him," Mallory offered.

"Right," Jared said. "She climbed after him. And then the cat jumped into another tree and Simon climbed after it, but the branch broke and he fell in a stream."

"But his clothes aren't wet," their mother said, scowling.

"Jared means that *I* fell in the stream," Mallory said.

"And my *shoe* fell in the stream," said Simon.

"Yeah," Jared said. "Then Simon caught the cat, but then we had to get them out of the tree without him getting clawed up."

"It took a while," said Simon.

Their mother gave Jared a strange look, but she didn't yell. "You three are grounded for the rest of the month. No playing outside and no more excuses."

Jared opened his mouth to argue, but he

couldn't think of a single thing to say.

As the three of them trooped up the stairs, Jared said, "I'm sorry. I guess that was a pretty pathetic excuse."

Mallory shook her head. "There wasn't much you could say. You couldn't explain what really happened."

"Where did those goblins come from?" Jared asked. "We never even found out what they wanted."

"The Guide," Simon said. "That's what I started to tell you before. They thought I had it."

"But how? How could they know that we found it?"

"You don't think that Thimbletack would have told them, do you?" Mallory asked.

Jared shook his head. "He didn't want us to mess with the book in the first place."

Mallory sighed. "Then how?"

"What if someone was watching the house, waiting for us to find the book?"

"Someone or something," Simon added worriedly.

"But why?" Jared asked a little louder than he intended. "What's so important about the book? I mean—could those goblins even read?"

Simon shrugged. "They didn't really say why. They just wanted it."

"Thimbletack was right." Jared opened the door to the room he shared with his twin.

Simon's bed was neatly made, the sheets pulled back and the pillow plumped. But Jared's bed was ruined. The mattress hung from the frame, strewn with feathers and stuffing. The sheets had been ripped to ribbons.

"Thimbletack!" said Jared.

"I told you," said Mallory. "You should never have grabbed that stone."

End of
BOOK TWO

About TONY DiTERLIZZI . . .

A *New York Times* best-selling author, Tony DiTerlizzi created the Zena Sutherland Award–winning *Ted, Jimmy Zangwow's Out-of-This-World Moon Pie Adventure,* as well as illustrations in Tony Johnston's Alien and Possum beginning-reader series. Most recently, his brilliantly cinematic version of Mary Howitt's classic *The Spider and the Fly* was awarded a Caldecott Honor. In addition, Tony's art has graced the work of such well-known fantasy names as J.R.R. Tolkien, Anne McCaffrey, Peter S. Beagle, and Greg Bear as well as Wizards of the Coast's *Magic The Gathering*. He and his wife, Angela, reside with their pug, Goblin, in Amherst, Massachusetts. Visit Tony on the World Wide Web at www.diterlizzi.com.

and HOLLY BLACK

An avid collector of rare folklore volumes, Holly Black spent her early years in a decaying Victorian mansion where her mother fed her a steady diet of ghost stories and books about faeries. Accordingly, her first novel, *Tithe: A Modern Faerie Tale,* is a gothic and artful glimpse at the world of Faerie. Published in the fall of 2002, it received two starred reviews and a Best Book for Young Adults citation from the American Library Association. She lives in West Long Branch, New Jersey, with her husband, Theo, and a remarkable menagerie. Visit Holly on the World Wide Web at www.blackholly.com.

Tony and Holly continue to work day and night fending off angry faeries and goblins in order to bring the Grace children's story to you.

Bad things happen,
plots get thick
in the house
of Spiderwick. . . .

Take this creature
from the wood.
Can his rants
be understood?

Or this wood elf
tall and fair.
Can you trust him?
Do you dare?

Find book three.
The answer's there.

ACKNOWLEDGMENTS

Tony and Holly would like to thank
Steve and Dianna for their insight,
Starr for her honesty,
Myles and Liza for sharing the journey,
Ellen and Julie for helping make this our reality,
Kevin for his tireless enthusiasm and faith in us,
and especially Angela and Theo—
there are not enough superlatives
to describe your patience
in enduring endless nights
of Spiderwick discussion.

The text type for this book is set in Cochin.
The display types are set in Nevins Hand and Rackham.
The illustrations are rendered in pen and ink.
Production editor: Dorothy Gribbin
Art director: Dan Potash
Production manager: Chava Wolin

Her whole body began to tremble.

Tony DiTerlizzi *and* Holly Black

Simon and Schuster Books for Young Readers
New York London Toronto Sydney Singapore

SIMON & SCHUSTER BOOKS FOR YOUNG READERS
An imprint of Simon & Schuster Children's Publishing Division
1230 Avenue of the Americas, New York, New York 10020

 • Book design by Tony DiTerlizzi and Dan Potash • Manufactured in the United States of America

20 19 18 17 16

Library of Congress Cataloging-in-Publication Data
Black, Holly.
Lucinda's secret / Holly Black ; [illustrated by Tony DiTerlizzi]—1st ed.
p. cm. — (Spiderwick chronicles ; bk. 3)
Sequel to: The seeing stone.
Summary: With goblins, trolls, and the house boggart all trying to get them, the Grace children turn to Great-Aunt Lucinda for help.
ISBN 0-689-85938-4
[1. Brothers and sisters—Fiction. 2. Great-aunts—Fiction.
3. Supernatural—Fiction.] I. DiTerlizzi, Tony, ill. II. Title.
PZ7.B52878 Lu 2003
[Fic]—dc21
2003008849

For my grandmother, Melvina,
who said I should write a book just like this one
and to whom I replied that I never would
—H. B.

For Arthur Rackham,
may you continue to inspire others
as you have me
—T. D.

Table of
Contents

List of Full-Page
Illustrations

Dear Reader,

Over the years that Tony and I have been friends, we've shared the same childhood fascination with faeries. We did not realize the importance of that bond or how it might be tested.

One day Tony and I—along with several other authors—were doing a signing at a large bookstore. When the signing was over, we lingered, helping to stack books and chatting, until a clerk approached us. He said that there had been a letter left for us. When I inquired which one of us, we were surprised by his answer.

"Both of you," he said.

The letter was exactly as reproduced on the following page. Tony spent a long time just staring at the photocopy that came with it. Then, in a hushed voice, he wondered aloud about the remainder of the manuscript. We hurriedly wrote a note, tucked it back into the envelope, and asked the clerk to deliver it to the Grace children.

Not long after, a package arrived on my doorstep, bound in red ribbon. A few days after that, three children rang the bell and told me this story.

What has happened since is hard to describe. Tony and I have been plunged into a world we never quite believed in. We now see that faeries are far more than childhood stories. There is an invisible world around us and we hope that you, dear reader, will open your eyes to it.

HOLLY BLACK

Dear Mrs. Black and Mr. DiTerlizzi:

I know that a lot of people don't believe in faeries, but I do and I think that you do too. After I read your books, I told my brothers about you and we decided to write. We know about real faeries. In fact, we know a lot about them.

The page attached* to this one is a photocopy from an old book we found in our attic. It isn't a great copy because we had some trouble with the copier. The book tells people how to identify faeries and how to protect themselves. Can you please give this book to your publisher? If you can, please put a letter in this envelope and give it back to the store. We will find a way to send the book. The normal mail is too dangerous.

We just want people to know about this. The stuff that has happened to us could happen to anyone.

Sincerely,

Mallory, Jared, and Simon Grace

*Not included.

THE JUNKYARD
THE CAMP
THE BRIDGE
THE SPIDERWICK ESTATE
ROUNTREE STREET
DULAC DRIVE
THE GROVE

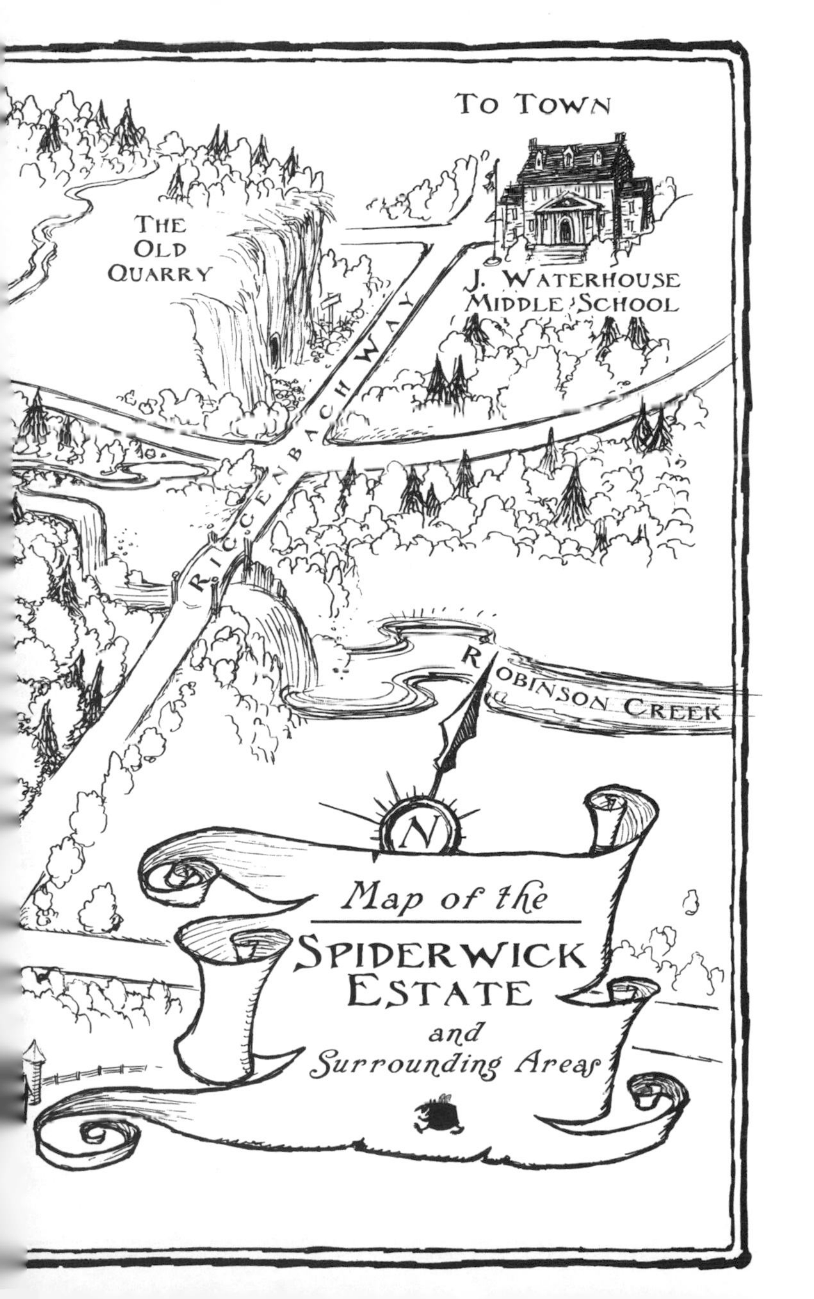
TO TOWN
THE OLD QUARRY
J. WATERHOUSE MIDDLE SCHOOL
RICCENBACH WAY
ROBINSON CREEK
N
Map of the
SPIDERWICK ESTATE
and
Surrounding Areas

THE
SPIDERWICK
CHRONICLES

Turned it inside out

Chapter One

IN WHICH Many Things Are Turned Inside Out

Jared Grace took out a red shirt, turned it inside out, and put it on backward. He tried to do the same with his jeans, but that was beyond him. *Arthur Spiderwick's Field Guide to the Fantastical World Around You* lay atop his pillow, open to a page on protective devices. Jared had consulted the book carefully, not sure any of it would help much.

Since the morning after the Grace kids had returned with the griffin, Thimbletack had been out to get Jared. Every so often he could hear the little brownie in the wall. At other times Jared thought he saw him out of the corner of his eye. Mostly, though, Jared just wound up the victim of some new prank. So far his eyelashes had been cut, his shoes had been filled with mud, and something had urinated on his pillow. Mom blamed Simon's new kitten for the last, but Jared knew better.

Mallory was completely unsympathetic. "Now you know how it feels," she kept saying. Only Simon seemed at all concerned. And he practically had to be. If Jared hadn't forced Thimbletack to give up the seeing stone, Simon might have been roasted over a spit in a goblin camp.

Jared tied the laces of his muddy shoe over an inside-out sock. He wished that he could find a way to apologize to Thimbletack. He'd tried to give back the stone, but the brownie hadn't wanted it. The thing was, he knew that if everything were to happen all over again, he would do exactly what he had done. Just thinking about Simon being held by goblins—while Thimbletack stood around talking in riddles—made Jared angry enough to almost break his laces with the force of the knot.

"Jared," Mallory called from downstairs. "Jared, come here a minute."

He stood up, tucking the Guide under his arm, and took a step toward the stairs. He fell immediately, hitting his hand and knee against the hardwood floor. Somehow Jared's shoelaces had been tied together.

Downstairs Mallory was standing in the kitchen, holding a glass up to the window so

The water caught the sunlight.

that the water caught the sunlight and cast a rainbow on the wall. Simon sat next to her. Both of Jared's siblings seemed transfixed.

"What?" Jared said. He was feeling grumpy and his knee hurt. If all they wanted was to show him how pretty the stupid glass looked, he was going to break something.

"Take a sip," Mallory said, handing the glass to him.

Jared eyed it suspiciously. Did they spit in it? Why would Mallory want him to drink water?

"Go ahead, Jared," Simon said. "We already tried it."

The microwave beeped and Simon jumped up to remove a giant mound of chopped meat. The top part was a sickly gray, but the rest of it still looked frozen.

"What's that?" Jared asked, peering at the meat.

"For Byron," Simon said, dumping it into a huge bowl and adding corn flakes. "He must be getting better. He's always hungry."

Jared grinned. Anyone else would be wary of a half-starved griffin recuperating in their carriage house. Not Simon.

"Go on," Mallory said. "Drink."

Jared took a sip of the water and choked. The liquid burned his mouth and he spat half of it onto the tile floor. The rest slid down his throat like fire.

"Are you crazy?" he yelled between bouts of coughing. "What was that?"

"Water from the tap," Mallory said. "It all tastes that way."

"Then why did you make me *drink* it?" Jared demanded.

Mallory crossed her arms. "Why do you think all this stuff is happening?"

"What do you mean?" Jared asked.

"I mean that weird things started happening when we found that book, and they're not going to stop until we get rid of it."

"Weird stuff was happening before we found it!" Jared objected.

"It doesn't matter," Mallory said. "Those

goblins wanted the Guide. I think we should give it to them."

The room was silent for a few seconds. Finally Jared managed a hushed, "What?"

"We should get rid of that stupid book," Mallory repeated, "before someone gets hurt—or worse."

"We don't even know what's wrong with the water." Jared glared at the sink, anger coiling in his gut.

"Who cares?" Mallory said. "Remember what Thimbletack told us? Arthur's field guide is too dangerous!"

Jared didn't want to think about Thimbletack. "We need the Guide," he said. "We wouldn't have even known there was a brownie in the house without it. We wouldn't have known about the troll or the goblins or anything."

"And they wouldn't know about us," Mallory said.

"It's mine," Jared said.

"Stop being so selfish!" Mallory shouted.

Jared clenched his teeth. How dare she call him selfish? She was just too chicken to keep it. "I decide what happens to it, and that's final!"

"I'll show you *final.*" Mallory took a step toward him. "If it wasn't for me, you'd be dead!"

"So?" Jared said. "If it wasn't for me, *you'd* be dead right back!"

Mallory took a deep breath. Jared could almost imagine steam coming out of her nose. "Exactly. We could all be dead because of that book."

The three of them looked down at "that book" dangling from Jared's left hand. He turned to Simon, furious. "I suppose you agree with her."

"We need the Guide."

Simon shrugged uncomfortably. "The Guide did help us figure out about Thimbletack and about the stone that lets you see into Faerie."

Jared smiled in triumph.

"But," Simon went on and Jared's face fell, "what if there are more goblins out there? I don't know if we could stop them. What if they got in the house? Or grabbed Mom?"

Jared shook his head. If Mallory and Simon destroyed the Guide, then everything they'd done would have been for nothing! "What if we give back the Guide and they keep coming after us?"

"Why would they do that?" Mallory demanded.

"We'd still *know* about the Guide," said Jared. "And we'd still know faeries are real. They might think we'd make another Guide."

"I'd make sure you didn't," said Mallory.

Jared turned to Simon, who was pushing a wooden spoon through the half-frozen mess of meat and cereal. "And what about the griffin? The goblins wanted Byron, didn't they? Are we going to give him back too?"

"No," said Simon, looking out of the faded curtains into the yard. "We can't let Byron go. He isn't all the way better."

"No one is looking for Byron," Mallory said. "It isn't the same thing at all."

Jared tried to think of something that would convince them, something that would prove that they needed the Guide. He didn't understand the faeries any more than Simon or Mallory did. He didn't even know why the faeries would *want* the field guide when the only thing in it was stuff about them. Did the faeries just not want *people* to see it? The only person who might know the answer was

Arthur and he was long dead. Jared stopped at that thought.

"There is someone we could ask—someone who really might know what to do," Jared said.

"Who?" asked Simon and Mallory in unison.

Jared had won. The book was safe—at least for now.

He smirked. "Aunt Lucinda."

It looked more like a manor than an asylum.

Chapter Two

IN WHICH Many People Are Mad

"It's very sweet of you kids to want to visit your great-aunt," Mom said, smiling into the rearview mirror at Jared and Simon. "I know she's going to love the cookies you made."

Outside the car window the trees streamed by, patches of yellow and red leaves between bare branches.

"They didn't *make* them," Mallory said. "All they did was arrange frozen dough on a pan."

Jared kicked the back of her seat, hard.

"Hey," Mallory said, turning around and

trying to grab her brothers. Jared and Simon snickered. She couldn't quite get them with her seat belt on.

"Well, that's more than you did," their mother said. "You are still grounded, young lady. All three of you have a week left."

"I was at fencing practice," Mallory said, slumping in her seat and rolling her eyes. Jared wasn't sure, but it seemed like there was something odd about the way her ears got pink when she said it.

Jared absently touched his backpack, feeling the outline of the field guide within, safe and sound, wrapped in a towel. So long as he kept it with him, there was no way that Mallory could get rid of it and no way the faeries could take it. Besides, maybe Aunt Lucinda knew about the Guide. Maybe she was the one who'd locked it up in the false bottom

of the chest for him to find. If so, maybe she could convince his brother and sister that it was important enough to keep.

The hospital where their great-aunt lived

was huge. It looked more like a manor than an asylum, with massive, redbrick walls, dozens of windows, and a neatly mown lawn. A wide, white stone path edged in rust-and-gold mums led to an entranceway cut from stone. At least ten chimneys rose from the black roof.

"Wow, this place looks older than our house," Simon said.

"Older," said Mallory, "but not nearly as crappy."

"Mallory!" their mother cautioned.

Gravel crunched under their tires as they pulled into the parking lot. Their mother chose a spot next to a battered, green car and turned off the engine.

"Does Aunt Lucy know we're coming?" Simon asked.

"I called ahead," said Mrs. Grace, opening the car door and reaching for her purse. "I don't know how much they tell her, though, so don't be disappointed if she's not expecting us."

"I bet we're the first visitors she's had in a long time," Jared said.

His mother gave him a *look*. "First of all, that is not a nice thing to say, and second, why are you wearing your shirt inside out?"

Jared looked down and shrugged.

"Grandma visits, doesn't she?" Mallory asked.

Their mother nodded. "She comes, but it's hard for her. Lucy was more like a sister than a cousin. And then when she started to . . . deteriorate . . . Grandma was the one who had to take care of things."

Jared wanted to ask what that meant, but something made him hesitate.

They walked through the wide, walnut doors of the institution. There was a desk in the vestibule, where a uniformed man was sitting, reading a newspaper. He looked up at them and reached for a tan phone.

"Sign in, please." He nodded toward an open binder. "Who're you here to see?"

"Lucinda Spiderwick." Their mother bent over the table and wrote their names.

At the sound of the name the man scowled. Jared decided right then that he didn't like this guy at all.

In a few minutes a nurse in a pink shirt with polka dots appeared. She led them through a maze of off-white hallways filled with stale air and the faint odor of iodine. They passed an empty room where a television flickered, and from somewhere nearby there was the sound of giddy laughter. Jared started to think of the asylums in movies and imagined wild-eyed people in straightjackets, biting at their bonds. He peered through the windowed doors they passed.

In one room a young man in a bathrobe giggled over an upside-down book, while in another a woman sobbed near a window.

Jared tried to avert his eyes from the next door, but he heard someone call, "My dancing partner is here!" Peering in, he saw a wild-haired man press his face against the window.

"Mr. Byrne!" The nurse stepped between Jared and the door.

"It's all your fault," the man said, showing yellow teeth.

"Are you okay?" Mallory asked.

Jared nodded, trying to pretend he wasn't shaking.

"Does that happen often?" Mrs. Grace asked.

"No," answered the nurse. "I'm very sorry. He's usually very quiet."

Before Jared could decide whether this visit was a good idea, the nurse stopped at a closed door, rapped twice, and opened it without waiting for a reply.

The room was small and the same not-quite-white color as the hallway. In the center of the room was a hospital bed with a metal headboard, and sitting up in it, with a comforter wrapped around her legs, was one of the oldest women Jared had ever seen. Her long hair was as white as sugar. Her skin was pale, too, almost transparent. Her back was hunched and twisted to one side. A metal stand by the side of her bed held a bag of clear liquid with a long tube that connected to the IV in her arm. But her eyes, when they focused on Jared, were bright and alert.

"Why don't I shut that window, Miss S.?" asked the nurse, moving past a nightstand cluttered with antique photos and knick-knacks. "You're going to catch a cold."

"No!" Lucinda barked, and the nurse stopped mid-stride. Then in a gentler voice their great-aunt continued. "Leave it be. I need fresh air."

"Hello, Aunt Lucy," Mom said hesitantly. "Do you remember me? I'm Helen."

The old lady nodded slightly, appearing to regain her composure. "Of course. Melvina's daughter. Goodness. You're quite a bit older than I remembered."

Jared noticed that his mother looked less than pleased by that observation.

"These are my sons, Jared and Simon," she said. "And this is my daughter, Mallory. We've been staying in your house and the children wanted to meet you."

Aunt Lucy frowned. "The house? It is not safe for you to stay at the house."

"We've had people in to make repairs," Mom said. "And look, the children brought some cookies."

"Lovely." The old woman looked at the plate as though it were piled with cockroaches.

Jared, Simon, and Mallory exchanged glances.

The nurse snorted. "Nothing you can do," the nurse said to Mrs. Grace, not seeming to care that Aunt Lucy could hear her. "She won't eat anything while we're watching."

Aunt Lucy narrowed her eyes. "I am not deaf, you know."

"You won't try one?" Mom asked, uncovering the sugar cookies and holding the platter out to Aunt Lucinda.

"I'm afraid not," said the old woman. "I find that I am quite content."

"Tell me what's happened."

"Perhaps we could talk in the hall," their mother whispered to the nurse. "I had no idea things were still so bad." With a worried look she put the plate on a side table and left the room with the nurse.

Jared grinned at Simon. This was even better than they had hoped. Now they were guaranteed at least a few minutes alone.

"Aunt Lucy," Mallory said, speaking fast. "When you told our mom that the house was dangerous, you didn't mean the construction, did you?"

"You meant the faeries," said Simon.

"It's okay to tell us. We've seen them," Jared put in.

Their aunt smiled at them, but it was a sad smile. "Faeries are *exactly* what I meant," she said, patting the bed beside her. "Come. Sit down, you three. Tell me what's happened."

"Come, my dears."

Chapter Three

IN WHICH Stories Are Told and a Theft Is Discovered

"We've seen goblins and a troll and a griffin," Jared told her eagerly as they arranged themselves at the foot of the hospital bed. It was such a relief to be believed. Now if she would just explain how important the Guide was, everything would be okay.

"And Thimbletack," Mallory put in, picking up a cookie and taking a bite. "We've seen him, although we're not sure if he counts as a brownie or a boggart."

"Right," said Jared. "But we need to ask you something important."

"Thimbletack?" Aunt Lucinda asked, patting Mallory's hand. "I haven't seen him in ages. How is he? The same, I expect. They're all always the same, aren't they?"

"I . . . I don't know," Mallory said.

Aunt Lucy reached into the drawer on her side table and brought out a worn, green cloth bag embroidered with stars. "Thimbletack loved these."

Jared took the bag and peered into it. Silvery jacks next to several stone and clay marbles glinted inside the pouch. "They're his?"

"Oh, no," she said. "They're mine, or they were, when I was young enough to play with such things. I'd just like him to have them. The poor thing, all alone in that old house. He must be so glad you've come."

Jared didn't think Thimbletack was all that glad, but he didn't say so.

"Was Arthur your dad?" Simon asked.

"Yes. Yes, he was," she said with a sigh. "Have you seen his paintings in the house?"

They nodded.

"He was a wonderful artist. He used to illustrate advertisements for soda pop and women's stockings. He made paper dolls for Melvina and me. We had a whole folder of them, with different dresses for each season. I wonder what ever happened to those things."

Jared shrugged. "Maybe they're in the attic."

"It doesn't matter. He's been gone for a long time now. I'm not sure I'd want to see them anyway."

"Why not?" Simon asked.

"Brings back memories. He left us, you know." She looked down at her thin hands. They were trembling. "He went out for a walk one day and never came back. Mother said she had known he was going to leave for a long time."

Jared was surprised. He'd never given much thought to what Uncle Arthur was like. He thought of the stern, bespectacled face in the library painting. He'd wanted to like his great-great-uncle, who could draw and see faeries. But if what Lucinda said was true, then he didn't like Arthur at all.

"Our dad left too," said Jared.

"I just wish I knew *why*." Aunt Lucy turned

her head away, but Jared thought he saw the glint of tears in her eyes. She pressed her hands together to make them stop shaking.

"Maybe he had to move for his job," Simon offered. "Like our dad."

"Oh, come on, Simon," Jared said. "You can't really believe that load of crap."

"Shut up, morons." Mallory glared at them. "Aunt Lucy, how come you're in this hospital? I mean, you're not crazy."

Jared winced, sure that Aunt Lucy would

be mad, but she only laughed. His anger faded.

"After Father left, Mother and I moved one town over to live with his brother. I grew up alongside my cousin Melvina—that's your grandmother. I told her about Thimbletack and about the little sprites, but I don't think she ever really believed me.

"Mother died when I was only sixteen. A year later I moved back into the estate. I tried to use what little money there was to fix the place up. Thimbletack was still there, of course, but there were other things too. Sometimes I saw shapes skulking around in the dark. Then one day they stopped hiding. They thought I had Father's book. They would pinch me and poke me and insist that I give it to them. But I didn't have it. Father had taken it with him. He never would have left it behind."

Jared started to speak, but his aunt was lost in her memories and didn't seem to notice.

"One night the faeries brought me a piece of fruit—just a little thing—the size of a grape and red as a rose. They promised not to hurt me anymore. Stupid girl that I was, I took the fruit and sealed my fate."

"Was it poison?" Jared asked, thinking of Snow White and apples.

"Of a fashion," she said with a strange smile. "It tasted better than any food I'd ever imagined. It tasted the way I thought flowers might. It tasted like a song you can't quite put a name to. After that, human food—normal food—was like sawdust and ashes. I couldn't make myself eat it. I would have starved."

"But you didn't starve," Mallory said.

"Thanks to the sprites who I played with when I was a child. They fed me and kept me

Creatures the size of walnuts

safe." Aunt Lucy smiled beatifically and stretched out one hand. "Let me introduce you. Come, my dears, come and see my niece and nephews."

There was a buzzing outside her open window and what had seemed like floating dust in the sunlight suddenly became creatures the size of walnuts, whirring in on iridescent wings. They alighted on the old woman, tangling in her white hair and crawling up the headboard.

"Aren't they darling?" their aunt asked. "My sweet little friends."

Jared knew what they were—sprites, like the ones in the woods—but that didn't make it any less eerie to watch them swarm over his aunt. Simon, however, seemed transfixed.

Mallory spoke, breaking the hush that had settled over them. "I still don't understand who put you here."

"Oh yes, the hospital," said Aunt Lucy. "Your grandmother Melvina became convinced I wasn't well. First she saw the bruises and then the lack of appetite. Then something happened. I don't want to frighten you—no, that's not quite true. I do want you to be frightened. I want you to understand how important it is for you to get out of that house.

"See these marks?" The old woman held out one thin arm. Scars ran deep in her flesh. Simon gasped. "Late one night the monsters came. Little green things with horrible teeth held me down, while a giant one questioned me. I struggled, and their claws scraped my arms and legs. I told them there was no book, that my father had taken it, but nothing I said made any difference. Before that night, my back was straight. Ever since, I have walked hunched over.

"The marks were the final straw for Melvina. She believed I was cutting myself. She couldn't understand . . . so she sent me here."

One of the faeries, clad only in a spiky, green seedpod, flew close and dropped a piece of fruit on the blanket near Simon. Jared blinked—he had been so wrapped up in the story, he'd nearly forgotten about them. The fruit smelled of fresh grass and honey and was enclosed in a papery skin, but underneath Jared could see the red flesh. Aunt Lucinda stared at it and her lips began to tremble.

"For you," said the little faeries in a unified whisper. Simon picked up the fruit and held it between his fingers.

"You're not going to eat it, are you?" Jared asked. Just looking made his mouth water.

"Of course not," said Simon, but his eyes gleamed greedily.

"You're not going to eat it, are you?"

"Don't," said Mallory.

Simon brought the faerie fruit closer to his mouth, still turning it. "One bite, just one little taste, wouldn't hurt," he said softly.

Aunt Lucinda's hand shot out and plucked the fruit from Simon's fingers. She popped it into her mouth and closed her eyes.

"Hey," said Simon indignantly, jumping up. Then he looked around, disoriented. "What just happened?"

Jared looked at their great-aunt. Her hands were shaking, even as she clasped them in her lap.

"They mean well," she said. "They just don't understand the craving. To them it is only food."

Jared looked at the little faeries. He wasn't sure what they knew or didn't know.

"But now you see why the house is too

dangerous for you children. You must get your mother to understand, to leave. If they know you're there, they'll think you have the Guide, and they will never leave you in peace."

"But we do have the Guide," Jared said. "That's what we came here to ask you about."

Aunt Lucy gasped. "You can't possibly—"

"We followed the clues in the library," Jared explained.

"See, she *does* think we should get rid of it!" Mallory said.

"The library? That means . . ." Aunt Lucy looked at him with dawning horror. "If you have the Guide, you have to get out of the house. Immediately! Do you understand me?"

"The Guide's right here." Jared unzipped his backpack and took out the towel-covered book. But when he unwrapped it, the field guide wasn't inside. They were all looking down at an old, worn copy of a cookbook, *Microwave Magic*.

Jared turned to Mallory. "You! You stole it!" He dropped the backpack and went at her with both fists.

Made their way into Arthur's library

Chapter Four

IN WHICH the Grace Children Look for a Friend

Jared pressed his face up to the car window and tried to pretend that he wasn't crying. The tears fell, hot against his cheeks. He let them run down the cool glass.

He hadn't actually hit Mallory. Simon had grabbed his arms while Mallory kept insisting that she hadn't taken the Guide. All the shouting had brought their mother in. She had dragged them out of there, with lots of apologizing to the nurse and even to Aunt Lucy, who had to be sedated. On the way to the car his mom had told Jared he was lucky the people at the institution didn't lock *him* up.

"Jared," Simon whispered, putting his hand on his twin's back.

"What?" Jared mumbled without turning.

"Maybe Thimbletack took it?"

Jared swiveled around in his seat. His whole body went tense. The moment he heard it, he knew it had to be true. It was Thimbletack's latest prank and his best revenge.

His insides felt as though they'd been splashed with ice water. Why couldn't he have figured that out for himself? Sometimes he got so angry that it scared him. It was like his mind went blank and his body took over.

When they got home, he slid out of the car and sat down on the back steps instead of going into the house with his mother. Mallory sat down beside him.

"I didn't take it," she said. "Remember when we believed you? Now you better believe me."

"I know," Jared replied, looking down. "I think it was Thimbletack. I . . . I'm sorry."

"You think Thimbletack stole the Guide?" she asked.

"Simon figured it out," said Jared. "It

makes sense. Thimbletack keeps playing pranks on me. This is just the worst one yet."

Simon sat down next to Jared on the stairs. "It'll be okay. We'll find it."

"Look," Mallory said, picking at the hem of her sweater where a thread had unraveled. "It's probably for the best."

"No, it's not," Jared said. "Even you should see that. We can't give back what we don't have! The faeries didn't believe Aunt Lucinda when she said she didn't have the book—why would they believe us?"

Mallory scowled and didn't answer.

"I was thinking," Simon said. "Aunt Lucy said that her dad abandoned them, right? But if the field guide was still hidden in the house, maybe he didn't leave on purpose. She said he would never take off without it."

"Then how come the book was still hidden?"

Jared asked. "If faeries captured him, he'd have told them where it was."

"Maybe he split before any faeries could catch him," Mallory said. "Let Lucy catch all the heat. Maybe he knew about the giant thing."

"Arthur wouldn't do that," Jared said. As soon as he said it, however, he wondered if it was true.

"Come on," said Simon. "We're never going to figure this out. Let's go visit Byron. He's probably hungry again, and it will get our minds off the Guide."

Mallory snorted. "Yeah, visiting a griffin living in our barn will definitely make us forget all about a book of supernatural creatures."

Jared smiled vaguely. He couldn't stop thinking about the book, about Aunt Lucy and Arthur, and about himself and Mallory and the anger he didn't know what to do with.

Jared looked over at her. "I'm sorry I tried to hit you."

Mallory ruffled his hair and stood up. "You hit like a girl anyway."

"I do not," Jared said, but he got up and followed her and Simon inside with a grin.

An old, yellowed piece of paper was lying on the kitchen table. Jared took a step closer. A poem had been scribbled on it.

"Thimbletack," Jared said.

Rash child who thinks he's smart
Wondering about your book?
Maybe I'm tearing it apart
Or hiding it where you won't look.

"Wow, he's really mad," said Simon.

Jared was torn between relief and horror. The book *was* with Thimbletack, but what had

he done with it? Had it really been destroyed?

"Hey, I know," Mallory offered hopefully. "Aunt Lucy's jacks and marbles. We could leave them for him."

"I'll write a note." Simon turned over the paper and scrawled something on the back.

"What does it say?" Mallory asked.

Byron was sleeping.

"We're sorry," read Simon.

Jared eyed the note skeptically. "I'm not sure if that and a bunch of old toys will be enough."

Simon shrugged. "He can't stay mad forever."

Jared was afraid he could do exactly that.

Byron was sleeping when they went to check on him, his feathery sides heaving with each breath. His eyes darted back and forth beneath shut lids. Simon pointed out that they probably shouldn't try to wake him, so they left another plate of meat by his beak and walked back to the house. Mallory suggested a game, but Jared was too nervous to do anything except try to figure out where Thimbletack could have hidden the Guide. He paced the living room, trying to think.

Maybe it was like a riddle, with a way to solve the puzzle. He thought about the note again, turning it over in his mind, looking for clues.

"It can't be inside the walls." Mallory sat cross-legged on the couch. "It's too big. How could he get it in there?"

"There are lots of rooms we've never even been in," Simon said, perching next to her. "Lots of places we haven't looked."

Jared stopped mid-stride. "Wait. What about right in front of us?"

"What?" asked Simon.

"In Arthur's library! There are so many books up there, we would never notice it."

"Hey, that's true," Mallory said.

"Yeah," said Simon. "And even if the Guide isn't there—who knows what else we'll find."

The three went upstairs into the hall and

opened the closet door. Crouching down, Jared crawled through the secret passage underneath the lowest shelf and made his way into Arthur's library. The walls were lined with bookshelves, except for where a large painting of their great-uncle hung. Despite their many visits to the library, dust still covered most of the bookshelves, a testament to how few of the volumes had been inspected closely.

Mallory and Simon scrambled in behind him.

"Where do we start?" Simon asked, looking around.

"You take the desk," Mallory said. "Jared, you take that bookshelf, and I'll take the one over here."

Jared nodded and tried to brush off some of the dust on the first shelf. The books were as strange as he remembered from previous trips to the library: *Physiognomy of Wings, Impact of*

Scales on Musculature, Venoms of the World, and *Details of Draconite.* When Jared had first looked at them, however, there had been a kind of awe that was absent now. He felt numb. The book was gone, Thimbletack hated him, and Arthur wasn't the person he'd imagined. It was a cheat—all this magic. It seemed so great, but underneath, it was just as disappointing as everything else.

Jared glanced over at the painting of Arthur hanging on the wall. He didn't even *look* nice to Jared anymore. The Arthur in the painting was thin-lipped with a crease between his brows that Jared now figured was annoyance. He was probably thinking about leaving his family even then.

Jared's vision blurred and his eyes burned. It was stupid to cry over someone he'd never met, but he couldn't help it.

He didn't even look nice.

"Did you sketch this?" Simon called from the desk.

Jared wiped his face against his sleeve, hoping his twin didn't notice the tears. "Just toss it."

"No," Simon said. "It's good. It really looks like Dad."

Learning to draw had been another stupid idea. All it had done was get him in trouble at school for doodling instead of working. He walked to the desk and tore the drawing in half, crumpling it in his fists. *"Just toss it!"*

"Guys," Mallory said. "Come here."

Mallory held several rolled-up sheets of paper and two long, metal tubes. "Look." She knelt down and began unrolling pages on the floor.

The boys crouched around. There, sketched in pencils and painted in watercolors, was a map of their neighborhood. Some places didn't look quite right—there were more houses and more roads now—but there were a lot of places they still recognized. The notes, however, were a surprise.

There was a thin circle surrounding a stretch of forest behind their house, with letters printed inside the circle. "TROLL HUNTING TERRITORY," Simon read.

Mallory groaned. "If only we'd had this before!"

Along a stretch of road near an old quarry, DWARVES? was written, while a tree not far from the house was clearly marked SPRITES.

The boys crouched around.

The strangest thing, however, was a note on the edge of the hills, close to their house. It looked like it had been written hastily, as the handwriting was sloppy. It read, "September 14th. Five o'clock. Bring the remains of the book."

"What do you think it's about?" Simon asked.

"Could 'the book' mean the field guide?" Jared wondered aloud.

Mallory shook her head. "Could be, but the Guide was still here."

They looked at each other for a moment in silence.

"When did Arthur disappear?" Jared finally asked.

Simon shrugged. "Probably only Aunt Lucy would remember."

"So either he went to the meeting and never

came back," Mallory said, "or he took off and never went to the meeting at all."

"We have to show this to Aunt Lucinda!" Jared said.

His sister shook her head. "It doesn't prove anything. It'll just make her more upset."

"But maybe he didn't mean to leave," Jared said with a scowl. "Don't you think she deserves to know that?"

"Let's go and look ourselves," Simon said. "We can follow the map and see where it leads. Maybe there'll be some clue about what really happened."

Jared hesitated. He wanted to go. He had been on the verge of suggesting it himself when Simon had spoken. Yet now he couldn't stop himself from wondering if it was some kind of a trap.

"Following this map would be really, really

dumb," said Mallory. "*Especially* if we think something might have happened to him out there."

"That map is so old, Mallory," Simon said. "What could happen?"

"Famous last words," Mallory said, but she traced the hills on the map thoughtfully with her fingers.

"It's the only way we will ever find out anything," said Jared.

Mallory sighed. "I guess we could take a look. As long as it's daytime. But the first weird thing we see, we go back. Agreed?"

"Agreed," Jared said with a smile.

Simon started to roll up the map. "Agreed," he said.

A summer breeze blew across the hill.

Chapter Five

IN WHICH There Are Many Riddles and Few Answers

To Jared's surprise, their mother agreed to let them go for a short walk. She blamed their constant squabbling on being cooped up inside but, with a single stern look at Jared, made all three promise to be back before dark. Mallory grabbed her fencing sword, Jared got his backpack and a new notebook, and Simon brought a butterfly net from the library.

"What is that for?" Mallory asked as they crossed Dulac Drive, following the map.

"To catch things," Simon said, without looking at her directly.

"What kind of *things*? Don't you have enough animals?"

Simon shrugged.

"You bring home one new creature and I'm feeding it to Byron."

"Hey," Jared said, interrupting them. "Which direction?"

Simon studied the map, then pointed.

Simon, Mallory, and Jared made their way up the steep hillside. Trees were sparse, their trunks growing on a slant between patches of grass and moss-covered boulders. For a long while they just climbed, not really talking. Jared thought that this might be a nice place to bring his sketchbook sometime—but then he remembered that he'd given up on drawing.

Near the top of the hill the land leveled out and

the trees grew thicker. Simon turned around suddenly and started leading them back down the hill.

"Where are we going?" Jared asked.

Simon waved the map at him. "This is the way," he said.

Mallory nodded as though she didn't think it was unusual that they were retracing their steps.

"Are you sure?" Jared asked. "I don't think so."

"I'm *sure,*" Simon said.

Right then a summer breeze blew across the hill, and Jared thought he heard a chorus of laughter from beneath their feet. He stumbled and almost fell.

"Did you hear that?"

"What?" Simon asked, looking around nervously.

Jared shrugged. He was sure he had heard

something, but now there was only silence.

A little bit down the path Simon changed direction again. He started walking back up and to the right. Mallory followed amiably.

"Where are we heading now?" Jared asked. They were going up again, toward the top of the first hill, which was good—but they had been traveling at such an angle that Jared didn't think they could be anywhere close to the meeting spot on the map.

"I know what I'm doing," said Simon. Mallory followed without question, which bothered Jared almost as much as the zigzag pattern Simon was taking. He wished he had the Guide. He tried to go through the pages in his mind, looking for some explanation. He recalled something about people losing their way, even really close to home. . . .

Jared began to poke the grass he stepped on with his shoe. One tall weed scuttled to the side.

"Stray sod!" He thought of the entry in the Guide. Suddenly it made sense that only he had noticed they were going in the wrong direction. "Simon! Mallory! Turn your shirts inside out like mine!"

"No," Simon said. "I know the way. Why do you always have to boss me around?"

"It's a faerie trick!" Jared yelled.

"Forget it. You follow me for a change!"

"Just do it, Simon!"

"No! Didn't you hear me? No!"

Jared tackled his brother, causing both of them to land on the grass. Jared tried to rip off his brother's sweater, but Simon was hugging his arms to his sides.

"Stop it, both of you!" Mallory pushed them apart. Then, to Jared's surprise, she sat down on Simon and tugged off his sweater. He immediately noticed that she'd already turned her own inside out.

A strange expression came over Simon's face as his inside-out sweater was shoved back over his head. "Wow. Where are we?"

A peal of laughter rang out from above their heads.

"Most don't make it this far—or this near, depending," said a creature perched in the tree. It had the body of a monkey with short, blackish brown speckled fur and a long tail that curled around the branch on which it sat. A thick ruff of fur surrounded its neck, but its face was rabbity, with long ears and whiskers.

"Depending on what?" Jared asked. He wasn't sure if he should be amused or afraid.

Suddenly the creature swung his head upside down so that its ears brushed its belly and its chin pointed toward the sky. "Clever is as clever does."

Jared jumped.

Mallory swung her rapier out in front of her. "Stay where you are!"

"Goodness, a beast with a sword," it hissed. Swinging its head right-ways-round again, it

"Most don't make it this far."

blinked twice. "I wonder if it's mad. Swords haven't been the fashion for ages!"

"We're not beasts," said Jared defensively.

"What are you then?" asked the creature.

"I'm a boy," said Jared. "And, well, that's my sister. A girl."

"That's no girl," it said. "Where's her dress?"

"Dresses haven't been the fashion for ages," Mallory said with a smirk.

"We answered your questions," Jared said. "Now answer ours. What are *you*?"

"The Black Dog of the Night," declared the creature proudly, before its head spun around once more, peering at them with one eye open. "An ass or perhaps merely a sprite."

"What does that mean?" demanded Mallory. "It's just stupid."

"I think it's a phooka!" said Jared. "Yes, I remember now. They're shape shifters."

"Are they dangerous?" asked Simon.

"Very!" said the phooka, nodding vigorously.

"I'm not sure," Jared said, under his breath. Then, clearing his throat, he addressed the creature. "We were looking for some trace of our great-uncle."

"You've lost your uncle! How careless."

Jared sighed and tried to decide if the phooka was as crazy as it seemed. "Well, he's been gone a long time, actually. Close to seventy years. We're just hoping to find out what happened to him."

"Anyone can live that long—all they have to do is keep from dying. But I understand that humans live much longer in captivity than they do in the wild."

"What?" Jared asked.

"When looking for something," said the phooka, "one ought to be sure one wants to find it."

"Oh, never mind!" Mallory said. "Let's just keep going."

"Let's at least ask it what's in the valley up ahead," said Simon.

Mallory rolled her eyes. "Oh, yeah, like it's going to start making sense."

Simon ignored her. "Can you please tell us what's up ahead? We were following this map until we got turned around by the moving grass."

"If grass can move," said the phooka, "then a boy could find himself rooted in place."

"Please, please, just stop encouraging it," said Mallory.

"Elves," said the phooka, eyeing Mallory as though affronted. "Shall I be direct when I direct you into the direct path of the elves?"

"What do they want?" asked Jared.

"They have what you want and they want what you have," said the phooka.

Mallory groaned audibly.

"We said we'd turn back when things got weird." Mallory pointed at the phooka with her rapier. "And that thing is about as weird as it gets."

"But not bad." Jared looked toward the hills. "Let's go on a little farther."

"I don't know," Mallory said. "What about those grass things and us getting lost?"

"The phooka said that the elves have what we want!"

Simon nodded. "We're really close, Mal."

Mallory sighed. "I don't like this, but I'd rather we were the ones sneaking up on them."

They started walking down the hill, away from the road.

"Wait! Come back," called the phooka. "There is something I must tell you."

They turned back.

"What is it?" Jared asked.

"Bonny nonny bonny," said the phooka with precision.

"Is that what you wanted to tell us?"

"No, not at all," said the phooka.

"Well, what then?" Jared demanded.

"What an author doesn't know could fill a book," said the phooka. With that, his body toed its way up the tree until it was gone.

They stopped in a meadow.

The three children made their way slowly down the other side of the hill. As the trees thickened once more, they noticed how quiet the woods had become. No birds sang in the trees. There seemed to be only the rustle of grass and the snap of twigs under their feet.

They stopped in a meadow ringed by trees. At the center a single, tall thorn tree stood, surrounded by fat white-and-red toadstools.

"Uh," Jared said.

"Right. Weird. Let's get out of here," Mallory said.

But as they turned, the trees wove together, branches entwining with other branches, lacing into a fence of foliage that reached down to the earthen floor of the glade.

"Oh, crap," said Mallory.

Three beings stepped out.

Chapter Six

IN WHICH Jared Fulfills the Phooka's Prediction

Across the grove the branches parted and three beings stepped out from the trees. They were about Mallory's size, with freckled skin browned by sunlight. The first was a woman with apple green eyes and a green sheen across her shoulders and at her temples. Leaves were tangled in her tousled hair. The second was a man with what looked like small horns along his brow. His skin was flushed a deeper green than the woman's skin and he held a gnarled staff in his hands. The third elf had thick, red hair woven with red berries and two large seedpods that stuck up on either side of his head. His skin was brown, speckled with red at his throat.

"These are elves?" Simon asked.

"No one has followed this path for a long time," said the green-eyed elf as though no one had spoken. She held her head high, like one accustomed to being obeyed. "All who might have stumbled into this grove have been led astray. But here they are. How curious."

"The grass," Jared whispered to his brother.

"They must have it," the red-haired elf declared to his companions. "How else would they come this way? How else would they discover the means to stay on the path?" He turned to the three children. "I am Lorengorm. We would bargain with you."

"For what?" Jared asked, hoping his voice

Drawing created by Jared Grace.

wouldn't shake. The elves were beautiful, but the only emotion he could read on their faces was a strange hunger that unnerved him.

"You want your freedom," said the elf with what had looked like horns. Jared realized that they were actually leaves. "We want Arthur's book."

"Freedom from what?" Mallory asked.

The leaf-horned elf indicated the border of trees with one hand and smiled an unkind smile. "We will guest you until you tire of our hospitality."

"Arthur didn't give you the book. Why should we?" Jared hoped they couldn't tell that he was guessing.

The leaf-horned elf sniffed. "We have long known that mankind is brutal. Once, at least, humans were ignorant. Now we would keep knowledge of our existence from you to protect ourselves."

"You cannot be trusted. You cleave the forests." Lorengorm scowled and his eyes flashed. "Poison the rivers, hunt the griffins from the skies and the serpents from the seas. Imagine what you could do if you knew all of our weaknesses."

"But *we* never did any of those things!" said Simon.

"And no one even believes in faeries," Jared said. He thought of Lucinda. "No one sane, anyway."

Lorengorm's laugh sounded hollow. "There are few enough faeries left to believe in. We make our homes in the sparse forests left to us. Soon even those will be gone."

The green-eyed elf lifted one hand toward the woven wall of branches. "Let me show you."

Jared noticed all types of faeries,

sitting in the circle of trees, peering through the gaps in the wood. Their black eyes glittered, their wings buzzed, and their mouths moved, but none entered the grove. It felt like a trial, with the elves acting as both judge and jury. Then a few branches untwined and something else stepped through.

It was white and the size of a deer. Its fur was ivory and its long mane hung in tangles. The horn that jutted from its forehead was twisted to an end that looked sharp. It lifted its wet nose and scented the air. As it approached them the valley went quiet. Even the creature's own steps were noiseless. It didn't look at all tame.

Mallory stepped toward it, tilting her head slightly and extending her hand.

"Mallory," Jared warned. "Don't . . ."

But she was beyond hearing, stretching out

her fingers to pet the creature's flank. It stayed completely still, and Jared was afraid to even breathe as Mallory stroked the unicorn's side, then tangled her hand in its mane. As she did, the bone horn touched her forehead and her eyes closed. Then her whole body began to tremble.

"Mallory!" Jared said.

Beneath the lids Mallory's eyes darted back and forth, as though she were dreaming. Then she staggered to her knees.

Jared ran forward to grab her. Simon was only a step behind him. When Jared touched Mallory, he was drawn into the vision.

Everything soundless.

Knots of blackberry bushes. Men on horseback. Lean dogs with red tongues. A glimmer of white, and a unicorn bursts through the glade, legs already dark with mud. Arrows fly, burying themselves in white

Her whole body began to tremble.

flesh. The unicorn bellows and goes down in a cloud of leaves. Dog teeth rip skin. A man with a knife hacks the horn from the head while the unicorn is still moving.

The images came faster then, more disjointed. *A girl in a colorless gown, urged on by hunters, lures the unicorn closer. One stray arrow knocks her to the ground. She falls, pale arm slung over pale flank. Both are still. Then hundreds of gory horns, shaped into goblets, crushed into charms and powders. White pelts streaked with blood, stacked in a pile buzzing with black flies.*

Jared pulled free of the dream, his stomach heaving. To his surprise Mallory was crying, her tears darkening the white fur. Simon put an awkward hand on the unicorn's side.

The unicorn tipped its head forward, nuzzling Mallory's hair with its lips.

"It really likes you," Simon said. He looked a little annoyed. Animals usually liked him best.

Mallory shrugged. "I'm a girl."

"We know what you saw," the leaf-horned elf said. "Give us the Guide. It must be destroyed."

"What about the goblins?" demanded Jared.

"What of them? The goblins love your world," said Lorengorm. "Your machines and poisons have made a haven for their kind."

"You seemed fine with using them to try to take the book from us," Jared said.

"We?" asked the green-eyed elf, her eyes wide and her mouth hard. "You think that we would send such sentries? It is Mulgarath that commands them."

"Who is Mulgarath?" Mallory stood up, still petting the unicorn absently.

"An ogre," said Lorengorm. "He has been gathering goblins to him and making pacts

with dwarves. We think he wants Arthur Spiderwick's Guide for himself."

"Why?" Jared asked. "Don't you know everything that's inside it?"

The elves exchanged uncomfortable glances. Finally the leaf-horned elf spoke. "We make art. We do not feel the need to cut things apart to see what they're made of. What

Arthur Spiderwick did, none of our kind would do."

The green-eyed elf put a hand on the other elf's shoulder. "What he means is that there may be things in the Guide that we do not know."

Jared thought for a moment. "So you don't really care about humans getting Arthur's field guide. You just don't want Mulgarath to have it!"

"The book is dangerous in anyone's hands," said the green-eyed elf. "There is too much knowledge therein. Give it over to us. It will be destroyed and you will be rewarded."

Jared held out his hands. "We don't have it," he said. "We couldn't give it to you if we wanted to."

The leaf-horned elf shook his head and slammed the butt of his staff. "You lie!"

"We really don't have it," said Mallory. "Honest."

Lorengorm raised a single, red brow. "Then where is it?"

"We think the house brownie has it," Simon put in. "But we're not sure."

"You lost it?" The green-eyed elf gasped.

"Thimbletack probably has it," Jared said in a small voice.

"We have tried to be reasonable," said the leaf-horned elf. "Humans are faithless."

"Faithless?" Jared repeated. "How do we know we can trust *you*?" He snatched the map from Simon and held it up for the elves to see. "We found this. It was Arthur's. It looks like he came here and I guess he met you. I want to know what you did with him."

"We spoke with Arthur," said the leaf-horned elf. "He thought to trick us. He had sworn he would destroy the Guide, and he came to our meeting with a bag of blackened paper and ashes. But he lied. He had burned another book. The Guide remained unharmed."

"We honor our word," said the green-eyed elf. "Though it be bitter, we fulfill our pledges. We have no sympathy for those who would deceive us."

"What did you do?" asked Jared.

"We kept him from doing further harm," said the green-eyed elf.

"Now you have come," said the leaf-horned elf. "And you *will* bring us the Guide."

Lorengorm waved his hand, and pale roots crept from the ground. Jared cried out, but his voice was lost in the creaking of branches and shuffling of leaves. The trees were untwining, their limbs moving back into natural shapes.

But dirty, hairy roots climbed Jared's legs and held him.

"Bring us the Guide or your brother will remain trapped forever in Faerie," said the leaf-horned elf.

Jared had no doubt that he meant it.

"Jared, *help!*" Jared called.

Chapter Seven

IN WHICH Jared Is Finally Pleased to Have a Twin

Mallory leapt forward, brandishing her rapier. Simon held his net in awkward imitation. The unicorn shook its head, mane flying as it galloped noiselessly into the depths of the forest.

"Oh ho!" said the leaf-horned elf. "Now we see the true character of humans!"

"Let my brother go!" Mallory yelled.

Jared suddenly had an idea.

"*Jared,* help!" Jared called, hoping that Simon and Mallory would get the hint.

Simon just looked at him in confusion.

"Jared," said Jared, "you have to help me."

Then Simon smiled at him, his eyes lighting up with understanding. "*Simon,* are you okay?"

"I'm fine, *Jared.*" Jared pulled his leg against the grip of the roots with all his might. "But I can't move."

"We'll come back with the Guide, *Simon,*" Simon said, "and then they'll have to let you go."

"No," said Jared. "If you come back, they might keep us all hostage. Make them promise!"

"Our word is our bond," sniffed the green-eyed elf.

"You didn't give us your word," Mallory said, looking at her brothers with growing alarm.

"Promise that Jared and Mallory can leave the grove safely and that if they return, they will not be held against their will," said Jared.

Mallory looked ready to protest, but she remained silent.

The elves looked at the siblings with some hesitation. Finally Lorengorm nodded. "Let it be so. Jared and Mallory may go from this grove. They will not be held here against their will now or later. Should they not bring the Guide, we will keep their brother, Simon, for all time. He will remain with us, ageless, beneath the hill, for a hundred times a hundred years—and should he ever leave, one step on the ground will bring all the missing years on to him at once."

The real Simon shivered and took a step closer to Mallory.

"Go swiftly," said the elf.

Mallory looked searchingly at Jared. The tip of her rapier had dipped, but she was still

They turned and looked back at him.

holding it in front of her and she made no move to leave the grove. Jared tried to smile encouragingly, but he was scared and he knew it showed on his face.

Shaking her head, Mallory followed Simon. After a few paces they turned and looked back at him, then started climbing the steep hill. In a few minutes they were obscured by leaves. Jared spoke.

"You have to let me go," he said.

"And why is that?" asked the leaf-horned elf. "You have heard our promise. We will not release you until your brother and sister have brought us the Guide."

Jared shook his head. "You said you wouldn't release *Simon*. I'm Jared."

"What?" demanded Lorengorm.

The leaf-horned elf took a step toward Jared, his hands curled like claws.

Jared swallowed hard. "Your word is your bond. You have to let me go."

"Prove yourself, child," said the green-eyed elf. Her lips pressed in a thin line.

"Here." Jared shrugged off his backpack into his trembling hands. There, along the top, three letters were monogrammed into the red canvas: JEG. "See. Jared Evan Grace."

"Go," said the leaf-horned elf, speaking the word as though it were a curse. "Much may your freedom please you if we come upon you or your false-hearted siblings again."

With that, the roots untwined from Jared's legs. He ran from the grove as fast as he could. He did not look back.

As he reached the top of the hill, he heard laughter.

He looked up into the nearby trees, but there was no sign of the phooka. Still, Jared was only half surprised when its now-familiar voice spoke. "I see you didn't find your uncle. A pity. Were you a little less clever, perhaps you'd have had more success."

Jared shuddered and rushed down the other side of the hill, fast enough that he was barely able to stop from running out into the middle of the road. He crossed the street and

He heard laughter.

ran through the iron gates into his own front-yard, panting.

Mallory and Simon were waiting for him on the steps. His sister said nothing but embraced him in a very un-Mallory-like fashion. He let himself be hugged.

"I had no idea what you were going to do," said Simon with a laugh. "That was a great trick."

"Thanks for going along with it," Jared said with a grin. "The phooka said something to me on the way back."

"Anything that made any sense?" Mallory asked.

"Well, I was thinking," said Jared. "Remember how the elves said they'd keep me in Faerie?"

"Keep *you*?" asked Simon. "They said *Simon*."

"Yeah, but think of what they were going to *do*. They were going to keep me there forever. Ageless, remember? Forever."

"So you think . . ." Mallory's voice trailed off.

"When I was leaving, the phooka said that if I'd been less clever, I might have had more success finding my uncle."

"You mean Arthur could be trapped with

the elves?" asked Simon as they trudged up the steps to the house.

"I think so," Jared said.

"Then he's still alive," Mallory said.

Jared opened the back door and stepped into the mudroom. He was still shaking from his encounter with the elves, but the smile on his face grew. Maybe Arthur hadn't run out on his family. Maybe he was a prisoner of the elves. And maybe—if Jared was clever enough—Arthur could even be saved.

Daydreaming about rescue, he barely noticed the glimmer of silver at his feet before he fell. Something sharp pressed into Jared's thigh and outstretched hand. Simon tripped too, crashing onto Jared, and Mallory, only a couple of steps behind, went down on top of them both.

"Crap!" yelled Jared, looking around. The

floor was littered with jacks and marbles.

"Ow," said Simon, trying to squirm out from under his sister. "Get off me, Mal."

"Ow yourself," Mallory said, pushing herself to her feet. "I'm gonna kill that little boggart." She paused. "You know what, Jared? If we find Arthur's field guide, I say we keep it."

Jared looked back at her. "You do?"

She nodded. "I don't know about you two, but I'm tired of being bossed around by faeries."

End of
BOOK THREE

About TONY DiTERLIZZI . . .

A *New York Times* best-selling author, Tony DiTerlizzi created the Zena Sutherland Award–winning *Ted, Jimmy Zangwow's Out-of-This-World Moon Pie Adventure,* as well as illustrations in Tony Johnston's Alien and Possum beginning-reader series. Most recently, his brilliantly cinematic version of Mary Howitt's classic *The Spider and the Fly* was awarded a Caldecott Honor. In addition, Tony's art has graced the work of such well-known fantasy names as J.R.R. Tolkien, Anne McCaffrey, Peter S. Beagle, and Greg Bear as well as Wizards of the Coast's *Magic The Gathering*. He and his wife, Angela, reside with their pug, Goblin, in Amherst, Massachusetts. Visit Tony on the World Wide Web at www.diterlizzi.com.

and HOLLY BLACK

An avid collector of rare folklore volumes, Holly Black spent her early years in a decaying Victorian mansion where her mother fed her a steady diet of ghost stories and books about faeries. Accordingly, her first novel, *Tithe: A Modern Faerie Tale,* is a gothic and artful glimpse at the world of Faerie. Published in the fall of 2002, it received two starred reviews and a Best Book for Young Adults citation from the American Library Association. She lives in West Long Branch, New Jersey, with her husband, Theo, and a remarkable menagerie. Visit Holly on the World Wide Web at www.blackholly.com.

Tony and Holly continue to work day and night fending off angry faeries and goblins in order to bring the Grace children's story to you.

A boggart, then goblins,
now wood elves, oh my!
What else will the Grace kids
unearth by and by?

All eyes on Jared.
This magnet, for trouble,
will soon have his very own
twin seeing double.

And beneath the Old Quarry
just outside of town
lives a king with a kingdom.
But who wears the crown?

Be bold, keep reading,
but beware the path down.

ACKNOWLEDGMENTS

Tony and Holly would like to thank
Steve and Dianna for their insight,
Starr for her honesty,
Myles and Liza for sharing the journey,
Ellen and Julie for helping make this our reality,
Kevin for his tireless enthusiasm and faith in us,
and especially Angela and Theo—
there are not enough superlatives
to describe your patience
in enduring endless nights
of Spiderwick discussion.

The text type for this book is set in Cochin.
The display types are set in Nevins Hand and Rackham.
The illustrations are rendered in pen and ink.
Production editor: Dorothy Gribbin
Art director: Dan Potash
Production manager: Chava Wolin

"Behold, mortals, a beauty that will never fade."

Tony DiTerlizzi *and* Holly Black

Simon and Schuster Books for Young Readers
New York London Toronto Sydney

SIMON & SCHUSTER BOOKS FOR YOUNG READERS
An imprint of Simon & Schuster Children's Publishing Division
1230 Avenue of the Americas, New York, New York 10020

 • Book design by Tony DiTerlizzi and Dan Potash • Manufactured in the United States of America

12 14 16 18 20 19 17 15 13 11

Library of Congress Cataloging-in-Publication Data
Black, Holly.
The ironwood tree / Holly Black and Tony DiTerlizzi—1st ed.
p. cm.— (The Spiderwick chronicles ; bk. 4)
Summary: After Mallory is kidnapped at her fencing meet, Jared and Simon search for her near an old quarry and find themselves amidst dwarves and goblins.
ISBN-13: 978-0-689-85939-7
ISBN-10: 0-689-85939-2
[1. Dwarfs—Fiction. 2. Goblins—Fiction. 3. Brothers and sisters—Fiction. 4. Twins—Fiction. 5. Caves—Fiction.]
I. DiTerlizzi, Tony, ill. II. Title.
PZ7.B52878Sp 2004
[Fic]—dc22
2004007426

For my grandmother, Melvina,
who said I should write a book just like this one
and to whom I replied that I never would
—H. B.

For Arthur Rackham,
may you continue to inspire others
as you have me
—T. D.

Table of
Contents

List of Full-Page
Illustrations

Dear Reader,

Over the years that Tony and I have been friends, we've shared the same childhood fascination with faeries. We did not realize the importance of that bond or how it might be tested.

One day Tony and I—along with several other authors—were doing a signing at a large bookstore. When the signing was over, we lingered, helping to stack books and chatting, until a clerk approached us. He said that there had been a letter left for us. When I inquired which one of us, we were surprised by his answer.

"Both of you," he said.

The letter was exactly as reproduced on the following page. Tony spent a long time just staring at the photocopy that came with it. Then, in a hushed voice, he wondered aloud about the remainder of the manuscript. We hurriedly wrote a note, tucked it back into the envelope, and asked the clerk to deliver it to the Grace children.

Not long after, a package arrived on my doorstep, bound in red ribbon. A few days after that, three children rang the bell and told me this story.

What has happened since is hard to describe. Tony and I have been plunged into a world we never quite believed in. We now see that faeries are far more than childhood stories. There is an invisible world around us and we hope that you, dear reader, will open your eyes to it.

HOLLY BLACK

Dear Mrs. Black and Mr. DiTerlizzi:

I know that a lot of people don't believe in faeries, but I do and I think that you do too. After I read your books, I told my brothers about you and we decided to write. We know about real faeries. In fact, we know a lot about them.

The page attached* to this one is a photocopy from an old book we found in our attic. It isn't a great copy because we had some trouble with the copier. The book tells people how to identify faeries and how to protect themselves. Can you please give this book to your publisher? If you can, please put a letter in this envelope and give it back to the store. We will find a way to send the book. The normal mail is too dangerous.

We just want people to know about this. The stuff that has happened to us could happen to anyone.

Sincerely,

Mallory, Jared, and Simon Grace

*Not included.

THE JUNKYARD
THE CAMP
THE BRIDGE
THE SPIDERWICK ESTATE
ROUNTREE STREET
DULAC DRIVE
THE GROVE

TO TOWN
THE OLD QUARRY
J. WATERHOUSE MIDDLE SCHOOL
RICCENBICH WAY
ROBINSON CREEK
N
Map of the
SPIDERWICK ESTATE
and
Surrounding Areas

THE
SPIDERWICK
CHRONICLES

"It's an abandoned quarry."

Chapter One

IN WHICH There Is Both a Fight and a Duel

The engine of the station wagon was already running. Mallory leaned against the door, her everyday sneakers grungy against the bright white of her long fencing socks. Her hair was gelled and pulled back into a ponytail so tight that it made her eyes bulge. Mrs. Grace stood on the driver's side, her hands on her hips.

"I found him!" Jared panted, running up to join them.

"Simon," their mother called. "Where were you? We looked everywhere!"

"The carriage house," Simon said. "Taking care of the . . . uh, a bird I found." Simon looked uncomfortable. He wasn't used to having to lie. That was mostly Jared's job.

Mallory rolled her eyes. "Too bad Mom wouldn't leave without you."

"Mallory," their mother said, shaking her head in disapproval. "All of you—get in the car. We're going to be late already, and I still have to drop something off."

As Mallory turned to put her bag in the trunk, Jared noticed that her chest looked strange. Stiff and weirdly . . . big.

"What are you wearing?" he asked, pointing.

"Shut up," she said.

He snickered. "It's just that you look like you've got—"

"Shut up!" she said again, getting into the front seat of the car while the boys climbed in the back. "It's for protection, and I have to have it on."

Jared smiled against the window and watched the woods go by. There hadn't been any faerie activity in more than two weeks—even Thimbletack had been quiet—and occasionally Jared had to remind himself that it was real. Sometimes it seemed like everything could be explained away. Even the burning water had been dismissed as simply being from a contaminated well. Until the old plumbing could be connected to a central line, they used gallons of supermarket water without Mom thinking it was strange. But there was Simon's griffin, and *that* couldn't be explained by anything but Arthur's field guide.

"Stop chewing on your ponytail," their mother said to Mallory. "What is making you so jittery? Is this new team really that good?"

"I'm fine," Mallory said.

Back in New York she'd fenced in sweatpants and a team jacket chosen from a pile. There had been a guy who'd hold up his hand on your side if you had scored. But at the new school, fencers wore real uniforms and had electric rapiers wired to a scoring machine that flashed lights when someone got hit. Jared thought that was enough to make anyone jumpy.

Apparently their mother had another explanation. "It's that boy, isn't it? The one you were talking to on Wednesday when I picked you up."

"What boy?" Simon asked from the backseat, already starting to laugh.

"Be quiet," said their mother, but she answered anyway. "Chris, the fencing captain. He is the captain, isn't he?"

Their sister grunted noncommittally.

"Chris and Mallory sitting in a tree, K-I-S-S-I-N-G," Simon sang. Jared giggled, and Mallory turned toward the backseat, eyes narrowed.

"Want to lose all your baby teeth at once?"

"Don't listen to them," their mother said. "And *don't* worry. You're a smart, pretty girl and a great fencer. I bet he likes you."

"Mom!" Mallory groaned and sank lower in the front seat.

Their mother stopped at the library where she worked, dropped off some paperwork, and

"I bet he likes you."

returned to the idling car, somewhat out of breath.

"Come on! I can't be late," Mallory said, smoothing her hair back unnecessarily. "It's my first match!"

Their mother sighed. "We're almost there."

Jared resumed looking out the window in time to see what looked like a deep crater. They were driving over a stone bridge. The school bus never went this way.

"Simon, look! What's that?"

"It's an abandoned quarry," Mallory said impatiently. "Where people used to dig up rocks."

"A *quarry,*" Jared echoed. He remembered something from the map they'd found in their great-uncle Arthur's study.

"Think they found any fossils?" Simon asked, half crawling over Jared to look out the

window. "I wonder what dinosaurs lived in this area."

Their mother was already pulling the car into the school parking lot. She didn't answer.

Jared, Simon, and their mother climbed up onto the gymnasium bleachers while Mallory went to sit with her team. Already seated were a few other families and a smattering of people Jared recognized from school. A rectangular pad was spread out on the floor with lines taped on it. Mallory called it a *piste,* but Jared thought it just looked like a long, black mat. Behind it was a folding table where the scoreboard sat, its large, colored buttons making it look more like a game than something important. The director was fiddling with the wires, connecting them to a foil and testing the force needed to make the buzzer sound and the lights flash.

Mallory sat down on a metal chair at one

end of the *piste* and started unpacking her bag. Chris squatted down to talk with Mallory. The other team milled around the opposite end. All the uniforms were so white, they made Jared's eyes hurt.

Finally the director announced it was time for the first bout. He called two fencers up and made each of them strap a small receiver to the back of their pants, then attached cords to their foils. It all looked so professional. As the fencers began, Jared tried to recall what Mallory had said about the flashing lights, but he couldn't.

"This is stupid. I like fencing better without all this junk," Jared said to no one in particular.

Two matches later Jared had figured out that the colored lights meant that the hit was good, but the white light meant that the hit didn't count. Only hits in the chest counted. Which was dumb, really, Jared had always thought. Getting hit in the leg hurt plenty, and Jared had practiced with Mallory enough to know.

Finally Mallory was called to the mat. Her opponent—a tall boy called Daniel Something-or-Other—snickered as he put on his mask. He obviously had no idea what was coming.

Jared elbowed Simon as his brother put a pretzel into his mouth. "He's going to get it."

"Ow," said Simon. "Cut it out."

Mallory's ponytail bounced as she advanced. Her sword struck Daniel hard in the chest before he could parry. The director raised one hand, and the scoreboard lit up with a point for Mallory. Jared grinned.

Their mother was craning her whole body forward as if there were something to hear other than the clang of thin metal blades locked

"I like fencing better without all this junk."

in the pattern of attack, parry, and riposte. Daniel lunged desperately, too upset to control his advance. Mallory countered, turning her defense into an attack and scoring another point.

Their sister beat Daniel without being touched once. They saluted each other formally, and the boy took off his mask, red-faced and breathing hard. When Mallory's mask came off, she smiled, eyes slitted with satisfaction.

On the way back to the metal chairs the fencing captain gave Mallory a quick awkward hug. Jared couldn't see very well, but he could have sworn that Mallory's face flushed darker than it had been when she stepped off the mat.

The bouts went on, with Mallory's team doing pretty well. When it was the captain's turn to fence, Mallory cheered loudly. Unfortunately it didn't seem to help. He was defeated by a narrow margin. Slinking back to his seat, he walked past her without a word and shrugged off her attempts to talk to him.

When Mallory was called to the mat again, Chris didn't even look up.

Jared watched from the stands and scowled. His scowl deepened when he noticed a blond-haired girl in white fencing garb rooting through his sister's bag.

"Who's that?" Jared pointed.

Simon shrugged. "I dunno. She hasn't fenced yet."

Could the girl be a friend of his sister? Maybe she was just borrowing something? The furtive way the girl stopped when anyone from the team looked her way made Jared think she was stealing. But what would anyone want in a bag of Mallory's dirty socks and spare foils?

Clang of thin metal blades

Jared stood up. He had to do something. Didn't anyone else notice what was happening?

"Where are you going?" his mother asked.

"Bathroom," he lied automatically, even though his mother would be able to see him walking across the gym. He wished he could tell her the truth, but she would have made up some excuse for the girl. She thought the best of everyone, except him.

Jared climbed down the bleachers and, staying close to the wall, crossed the court to where the girl was still rummaging. But as Jared approached the chairs, the coach stopped him.

The fencing coach was wiry and short, with patchy white stubble on his face. "Sorry, kid, you can't come over here during the meet."

The coach stopped him.

"But that girl's trying to steal my sister's stuff!"

The coach turned. "Who?"

As Jared swung around to point her out, though, he realized that she'd disappeared. He fumbled for an explanation. "I don't know who she is. She hasn't fenced yet."

"Everybody's fenced, kid. I think you'd better go back to your seat."

Jared turned back to the bleachers, embarrassed, then thought better of it. He'd go out to the bathroom so that maybe his mother would ask fewer questions when he returned. Just before he walked through the blue gym doors, he stopped and looked back. Now *Simon* was fumbling through Mallory's bag. But Simon was wearing *his* clothes! Everyone would think it was him. He narrowed his eyes, wishing what he saw made sense.

Then a horrible suspicion formed in his mind. Glancing up into the stands, he caught sight of his brother sitting beside his mother, chewing on pretzels. Whatever that thing was, it wasn't Simon.

"Don't you know me?"

Chapter Two

IN WHICH the Grace Twins Are Triplets

Jared couldn't move from the doorway. He heard the clanging of swords and cheering, but the sounds seemed to come from far away. He watched in horror as the coach confronted his double. The man got red in the face, and some of the other players looked at Jared's double in shock.

"Great." Jared grimaced. There was no way he could explain this.

The coach pointed toward the large gym door, and he watched Not-Jared stalk toward it—and toward him. As Not-Jared got closer to Jared, it smirked. Jared clenched his hands into fists.

Not-Jared passed Jared without a single glance, slamming through the double doors. Jared wanted to find some way to wipe that smile off its face. He followed after it, into a hallway lined with lockers.

"Who are you?" Jared demanded. "What do you want?"

Not-Jared turned to face him, and something in its eyes made Jared go cold all over. "Don't you know me? Am I not your own self?" Its mouth curled into a sneer.

It was strange to watch it move and speak. It wasn't like watching Simon, with his tidy hair and the smear of toothpaste on his upper lip. And it wasn't quite himself either—the hair was messier, and the eyes were darker and . . .

different. It took a step toward him.

Jared took a step back, wishing for any kind of faerie protection, and then he remembered the pocketknife in his jeans. Faeries hated iron, and steel was at least part iron. He opened one of the blades. "Why don't you all just leave us alone?"

The creature threw back its head and laughed. "You can never get away from your own self."

"Shut up! You're not me." Jared pointed the knife at his double.

"Put that toy away," Not-Jared said, its voice low and harsh.

"I don't know who you are, or who sent you, but bet I know what you're looking for," said Jared. "The Guide. Well, you're never going to get it."

The creature's grin widened into something that still wasn't really a smile. Then suddenly it shrank back as though frightened. Jared watched in amazement as the Not-Jared's body shrank, its dark hair paled into a sandy brown, and its now blue eyes went wide with terror.

Before Jared could fully comprehend what he was seeing, he heard a woman's voice behind him.

"What's going on here? Put that knife down."

The vice principal rushed up, grabbing Jared's wrist. The pocketknife clattered to the linoleum floor. Jared stared at the blade as the sandy-haired boy ran off down the hall, his sobs sounding a lot like laughter.

"I can't believe you brought your knife to school," Simon whispered to Jared as they sat together outside the vice principal's office.

Jared shot him a look. He had explained several times—even once to the police—that he was only *showing* the kid the knife, but they'd never found the other boy to confirm the story. Then the vice principal had asked Jared to wait outside. Their mother had been in the vice principal's office a long time, but Jared couldn't hear what was going on.

"What kind of faerie do you think that thing was?" Simon asked.

"What kind of faerie do you think it was?"

Jared shrugged. "I wish we had the book so I could look it up."

"You don't remember anything that could shape-shift like that?"

"I don't know." Jared rubbed his face.

"Look, I told Mom it wasn't your fault. You'll just have to explain."

Jared gave a short laugh. "Yeah, like I can tell her what happened."

"I could say that kid stole something from Mallory's bag." When Jared didn't respond, Simon tried again. "I could pretend I did it. We could switch shirts and everything."

Jared just shook his head.

Finally their mother emerged from the vice principal's office. She looked tired.

"I'm sorry," Jared said.

He was surprised by the calm tone of her voice. "I don't want to talk about it, Jared.

Get your sister and let's just go."

Jared nodded and followed Simon, looking back just in time to see their mother sink down in the chair he'd vacated. What was she thinking? Why wasn't she yelling? He found himself wishing that she was mad—at least *that* he would understand. Her quiet sadness was more frightening. It was like this was all she *expected* of him.

Simon and Jared walked through the school, stopping to ask fencing team members if they'd seen Mallory. None of them had. They even stopped Chris-the-captain. He looked uncomfortable when they asked about Mallory, but he shook his head. The gymnasium was empty, the only sounds the echo of their steps on the glossy wood floor. The black mat had been rolled up, and everything from the meet had been put away.

Finally a girl with long, brown hair told them she'd seen Mallory crying in the girls' bathroom.

Simon shook his head. "Mallory? Crying? But she won."

The girl shrugged. "I asked her if she was okay, but she said she was fine."

"You think that was really her?" Simon asked as they walked toward the restroom.

"You mean, was something impersonating her? Why would a faerie turn into Mallory and then cry in a girls' bathroom?"

"I don't know," said Simon. "I'd cry if I had to turn into Mallory."

Jared snorted. "So, you want to go in there and look for her?"

"I'm not going into the girls' room," Simon said. "Besides, you're already in so much trouble, there's no way you can get into more."

"I can *always* get into more trouble," Jared said with a sigh. He pushed open the door. It looked surprisingly like the boys' room, except there were no urinals.

"Mallory?" he called. No answer. He peered under the stalls but didn't see any feet. He pushed open one of the doors gingerly. Even though there was no one in there, he felt weird, jumpy and embarrassed. After a moment he darted back out into the hall.

"She's not in there?" Simon said.

"It's empty." Jared glanced past the line of lockers, hoping no one had seen him.

"Maybe she went to the office looking for us," Simon said. "I don't see her anywhere."

A feeling of dread uncoiled in the pit of Jared's stomach. After the vice principal had caught him, he hadn't really thought about anything but how much trouble he was in. But

"Mallory?"

that thing was still running around the school. He remembered how the creature had looked through Mallory's bag at the match.

"What if she went outside?" Jared said, hoping that they could still find her before it did. "She could have gone out to see if we were waiting by the car."

"We could look." Simon shrugged. Jared could tell he wasn't convinced, but they walked outside anyway.

The sky had already deepened to purples and golds. In the dimming light they walked past the track and the baseball field.

"I don't see her," Simon said.

Jared nodded. His stomach churned with nervousness. *Where is she?* he wondered.

"Hey," Simon said. "What's that?" He walked a few feet and leaned down to pick up something shining in the grass.

"Mallory's fencing medal," Jared said. "And look."

On the grass large chunks of rock formed a circle around the medal. Jared knelt down beside the largest stone. Engraved deeply in the rock was a word: TRADE.

"Stones," Simon said. "Like from the quarry."

Jared looked up, surprised. "Remember the map we found? It said dwarves live in the quarry—but I don't think dwarves can shape-shift."

"Mallory could still be inside with Mom. She could be in the office waiting for us."

Jared wanted to believe it. "Then why is her medal out here?"

"Maybe she dropped it. Maybe this is a trap." Simon started walking back toward the school. "Come on," he said. "Let's go back and see if she's with Mom."

Jared nodded numbly.

When they got back inside, they found their mother in the school entrance, talking into her cell phone. Her back was to them, and she was alone.

Although their mother was speaking softly, her voice traveled easily to where they crouched. "Yeah, I thought things were getting better too. But, you know, Jared never admitted to what happened when we first moved here . . . and well, this is going to sound strange, but Mallory and Simon are so protective of him."

Jared froze, both dreading what she was going to say and unable to make himself do anything to stop her from continuing.

"No, no. They deny he ever did any of those things. And they're keeping something from me. I can tell by the way they stop talking when they come into a room, the way they cover for one another, especially for Jared. You should have heard Simon tonight, making up excuses for his brother pulling a knife on that little boy." Here she made a choked noise and began crying.

"I just don't know if I can handle him anymore. He is so angry, Richard. Maybe he should go and stay with you for a while."

Jared froze.

Dad. She was talking to their dad.

Simon jabbed Jared in the arm. "Come on. Mallory's not here."

Jared turned dazedly and followed his brother out the door. He could not have said how he felt at that moment—except maybe hollow.

SEEM TO TRICK HEN TOOK PEN

Chapter Three

IN WHICH Simon Solves a Riddle

"What are we going to do?" Simon asked as they walked back down the hallway.

"They have her," Jared said softly. He had to blot out what he'd just heard, blot everything from his mind except Mallory. "They want to trade her for the Guide."

"But we don't have it."

"Shhh!" Jared said. He had an idea, but he didn't want to say it aloud, out in the open air. "Come on."

Jared went to his locker and got a towel

from his gym bag. He picked out a textbook—*Advanced Mathematics*—that was about the same size as the Guide and folded it in the cloth.

"What are you doing?"

"Here," he whispered, shoving the wrapped package at Simon. He grabbed his backpack from the locker. "Thimbletack fooled us with this trick. Maybe we can fool whoever took Mallory."

Simon nodded once. "Okay, I think Mom has a flashlight in the car."

They clambered over a chain-link fence at the edge of the schoolyard and crossed the highway. The other side of the road was overgrown with weeds. It was hard to walk in the dark, and the flashlight gave off only a faint narrow light.

They climbed over a large pile of rocks, some covered in slick moss, others cracked in parts. As they went, Jared couldn't stop replaying what he'd overheard. He thought about the awful things that his mother believed and the even more-awful things she was likely to believe now that he'd disappeared. No matter what he did, he wound up in deeper and deeper trouble. What if he were expelled? What if she were to send him out to live with his dad, who wouldn't want him?

"Jared, look," said Simon. They had come to the edge of the old quarry.

The rock had been mined jaggedly; chunks of stone stuck out like ledges along the nearly thirty-foot drop to the uneven valley below. Scrubby bits of grass grew along the walls from thick veins of dirt. The highway ran over the top of the cavern, elevated on a thick stone bridge.

"It's weird to mine rocks, isn't it?" Simon asked. "I mean, they're just *rocks*.

"Probably granite," he continued when Jared didn't answer. Simon wrapped his thin jacket tighter around himself.

Jared shone his flashlight along the walls, catching a streak of rust and a blush of ochre in the beam. He had no idea what kind of stone it was.

Simon shrugged. "So, uh, how are we going to get down there?"

"I don't know. Why don't you tell me, if you know so much?" Jared snapped.

"We could . . . ," Simon started, but he trailed off and Jared felt bad.

"Let's just try to climb down," said Jared, pointing. "We can jump to that ledge and then try to get to another one."

"That's pretty far down. We should get a rope or something."

"That's pretty far down."

"We don't have time," Jared said. "Here, hold the light."

Thrusting the metal cylinder into his twin's hands, Jared sat on the edge of the cliff. Without the flashlight, when he looked down, he saw only the deep darkness below. Taking a breath, he scooted off, letting himself drop to a stone shelf he could not see.

Turning, he started to stand. Light shone in his eyes, blinding him. He stumbled and fell forward.

"Are you all right?" Simon called.

Jared shaded his face and tried to keep calm. "Yeah. Come on. Your turn."

He heard the crunching of dirt above him as Simon got into position. Quickly Jared moved out of the way, feeling ahead of him for an edge he only dimly remembered. Simon landed heavily beside him with a yelp.

The flashlight tumbled from Simon's hands

and fell into the darkness, hitting the valley floor hard, bouncing once and then lying still, illuminating a thin path of scrub and stone.

"How could you be so dumb!" Jared felt his temper like it was a living thing inside him, growing by the minute. Only shouting seemed to keep it from overwhelming him. "Why didn't you throw

it down to me? How are we going to climb down in the dark? What if Mallory's in danger? What if she *dies* because you were such a moron?"

Simon's head came up, his eyes shining with tears, but Jared was as shocked as his brother.

"I didn't mean it, Simon," he said hastily.

Simon nodded, but turned his face away from Jared.

"I think there's another ledge there. See that shape?"

Simon still didn't say anything.

"I'll go first," Jared said. He took a deep breath and dropped into the blackness. He hit the second ledge hard—it must have been farther down than he'd thought. His breath was knocked out of him, and his hands and knees were on fire. Slowly he pushed himself upright. His jeans were ripped widely over one knee, and his arm had a cut that started to bleed sluggishly. But from there it was only a short hop down to the quarry floor.

"Jared?" Simon's voice came faintly from where he was still sitting on the top ledge.

"I'm here," Jared called. "Don't move. I'll get the light."

He crawled over to grab the flashlight and turned it toward his brother, searching out ledges where Simon could step or niches he could grab. Slowly Simon climbed his way to the ground. But as he waited, Jared noticed echoing sounds, a distant thrum and a pounding that seemed to come from nowhere and everywhere at once.

Shining the flashlight around the quarry, he saw more jagged rock with faint traces of drill lines. He now wondered how they were ever going to get out. But before he had time to worry about that, the light flashed on an overhang of rock on the wall. As the light passed over the stone, a mottled pattern of fungi gave off a dim bluish glow.

"Bioluminescence," Simon said.

"Huh?" Jared took a step closer.

"When something makes its own light."

By the weak glow, Jared saw that a rectangle of stone under the ledge had been carved with a pattern of intertwining grooves. Looking at the center of the rock, he could make out the tops of letters hewn into the stone. He turned the flashlight directly on them.

SEEM TO TRICK HEN TOOK PEN

"A riddle," said Jared.

"It doesn't make any sense," said Simon.

"Who cares about that? How do we solve it?" They didn't have time to stand around now. They were almost inside, almost to Mallory.

"You solved the one back at the house," said Simon, sitting down with his back to his brother. "You figure it out."

Jared took a deep breath. "Look, I'm really sorry about what I said before. You have to help," Jared pleaded. "Everyone knows you're smarter than I am."

Simon sighed. "I don't understand the riddle either. A hen is a girl chicken, right? And a pen could be the place where they keep chickens. I don't know about the rest."

Jared looked at the words again. He couldn't seem to concentrate. What trick could a chicken perform? Maybe they were supposed to offer eggs at the entrance? Did the Guide say anything about chickens and faeries? He wished he had the book now. . . .

"Hey, wait a minute," Simon said, turning around and kneeling up. "Give me that light."

Jared handed over the flashlight and watched as Simon scratched out the message in the thin dirt with his finger. Then he started scratching out certain letters and writing them above in a different pattern.

MITES OPEN THREE TOCK KON

"What are you doing?" Jared sat down beside his twin.

SUSPENSION/EXPULSION FORM

J. WATERHOUSE MIDDLE SCHOOL

DATE: October 11

STUDENT NAME: Grace, Jared

SEX: M GRADE: 4 AGE: 9 SSN: 134-00-2067

STUDENT LIVES WITH: x Mother ___Father ___Both ___Other

Jared Grace HAS BEEN SUSPENDED FROM J. WATERHOUSE MIDDLE SCHOOL FOR A PERIOD OF 10 DAYS.

DURING THIS TIME, THE STUDENT IS BANNED FROM CAMPUS AND ALL SCHOOL FUNCTIONS
THIS IS THE STUDENT'S first SUSPENSION AND IS FOR THE FOLLOWING REASONS:
On October the eleventh, Jared Grace was seen in the hallway during an athletic event, threatening another child with a knife. In accordance with our policy, any student who is found on school premises, at school-sponsored or school-related events, in possession of a dangerous weapon (see chapter 55C for what constitutes a dangerous weapon under the school guidelines) or controlled substance may be subject to expulsion from the school or school district.

WE REGRET THAT IT IS NECESSARY TO TAKE THIS DISCIPLINARY ACTION. IF YOU DESIRE FURTHER INFORMATION ON THIS MATTER, YOU MAY CONTACT ME DIRECTLY AT THE SCHOOL.

GRADED SCHOOLWORK MISSED BY A STUDENT ON AN OUT-OF-SCHOOL SUSPENSION CANNOT BE MADE UP.

WE ARE HOPEFUL OUR COORDINATED EFFORTS WILL LEAD TO A BETTER UNDERSTANDING AND SOLUTION TO THE PROBLEM.

COMMENTS:
Due to previous disciplinary problems in the classroom here and at his previous school as well as the serious nature of this incident, expulsion is recommended. A hearing before the school board will be scheduled. You and your son are encouraged to attend and present any information you feel will be material to a decision on this matter.

THE ABOVE NAMED STUDENT HAS BEEN AFFORDED DUE PROCESS AND ALL SUSPENSION/EXPULSION PROCEDURES HAVE BEEN FOLLOWED AS DIRECTED BY STATE L

PRINCIPAL'S SIGNATURE

Carbon copy of Jared Grace's expulsion letter.

"I think you have to rearrange the letters to get the real message. Like those puzzles in the paper that Mom is always doing." Simon inscribed a third phrase in the dust.

KNOCK THREE TIMES TO OPEN

"Wow," said Jared. He couldn't believe that Simon had figured it out. He never would have solved it.

Simon grinned. "Easy," he said, walking up to the door and knocking three times on the hard stone face.

Just then the ground shifted underneath them, and both twins fell into the chasm that opened beneath their feet.

"What have we here? Prisoners!"

Chapter Four

IN WHICH the Twins Discover a Tree Unlike Any Other

They tumbled down into a net of woven metal. Yelping and kicking, Jared tried to stand, but he couldn't seem to get a foothold. Abruptly he stopped struggling and got elbowed in the ear by his brother.

"Simon, stop! Look!"

Glowing fungi covered the walls in patches, illuminating the faces of three small men with skin as gray as stone. Their clothes were drab and sewn from rough fabrics, but their silver bracelets, crafted in the shape of serpents, were so intricate that they seemed to slither around the men's thin arms; their collars were woven with golden threads beaten so fine that they might have been cloth; and their jeweled rings were so lovely that each of their dirty fingers gleamed.

"What have we here? Prisoners!" said one with a voice like gravel. "Seldom have we any live prisoners."

"Dwarves," Jared whispered to his brother.

"They don't seem very 'hi-ho, hi-ho,'" Simon whispered back.

The second dwarf rubbed several strands of Jared's hair between his fingers and turned to the one who had spoken. "Not very extraordinary, are they? The black of their tresses is dull and plain. Their skin is neither smooth nor pale as marble. I find them ill made. We could do far better."

Jared scowled, not sure what the dwarf meant. Again, he wished for the Guide. He remembered only that dwarves were great craftspeople, and the iron that hurt other faeries didn't bother them. His knife would have been useless, even if it hadn't been confiscated.

"We're here for our sister," Jared said. "We want to trade."

One of them chuckled, but Jared wasn't sure which. With a creak another dwarf positioned a silvery cage beneath the netting.

"The Korting said you would come. He is very eager to meet you."

"Is he like the dwarf king or something?" Simon asked.

The dwarves did not answer. One pulled on a carved handle and the net opened. Both boys fell heavily into the cage. Jared's hands and knees felt raw all over again. He slammed his fist against the metal floor.

Jared and Simon were silent as they were wheeled through caverns with cold air and wet walls. They could hear the sounds of hammers, louder and more distinct now that they were underground, and the roaring of what might have been a great fire. Overhead in the gloom, patches of dim phosphorescence showed the tips of large stalactites, hanging above them like a forest of icicles.

They passed through a grotto where bats shrieked from above, and the floor was dark and rank with their droppings. Jared tried to contain a shiver. The deeper they went, the colder the cavern became. Sometimes Jared saw shadows shift in the gloom and heard an erratic tapping.

As they moved through a narrow corridor, past dripping columns, Jared breathed in the damp, mineral scent with relief after the stink of the bats. The next chamber seemed to be filled with dusty piles of metal objects. A golden rat with sapphire eyes darted out of a malachite goblet and watched them pass. A silver rabbit lay on its side, a winding key around its neck, while a single bud of a platinum lily opened, then closed, then opened again. Simon looked at the metal rat with longing.

Then they moved into a large cavern where they saw dwarves carving statues of other dwarves into the granite walls. The sudden brightness of the lantern light stung Jared's eyes, but as he passed the dwarves, he thought he saw one of the carving's arms move.

From there they moved into an enormous space where a massive tree grew underground. The thick trunk reached up until it was lost in the shadows, branches forming a canopy over them. The air was filled with a strange metallic birdsong.

"That can't be a tree," Simon said. "There's no sun. No sun means no photosynthesis."

Jared peered at the trunk. "It's metal," he said, realizing that the leaves were all of beaten silver. High in the tree a copper bird beat its mechanical wings and stared down with cold, jet eyes.

"The first ironwood tree," said one of the dwarves. "Behold, mortals, a beauty that will never fade."

Jared looked up at the tree with awe, amazed by how one metal had been forged as rough as bark and twisted into branches while another was as delicate as filigree. Each silver leaf was unique, veined and curled like a real one.

"Behold, mortals, a beauty that will never fade."

"Why do you call us mortals?" Jared asked.

"Don't you know your own tongue?" a dwarf said, and snorted. "It means one who is fated for death. What else should we call you? Your kind wither in a blink of the eye." He leaned close to the bars of the cage and winked.

Several passages led from the cavern out into corridors that were too dim for Jared to see where they led. The cage was wheeled through one—a wide, columned hallway that led into a smaller room. Sitting on a throne hewn from an enormous stalagmite was another gray-skinned man, this one with a wiry black beard. His eyes shone like green jewels. A metal dog stretched out on a deerskin rug before the throne, the dog's side rising and falling in time with a thin mechanical wheeze, just as if it were really sleeping. On its back a single key slowly turned.

"My lord Korting."

Around the throne were other dwarves, all of them silent.

"My lord Korting," said one of the dwarves. "It is as you said. They have come looking for their sister."

The Korting stood. "Mulgarath told me you would come. How fortunate you are to be here, how honored that you will see the beginning of the end of human rule."

"Whatever," Jared said. "Where's Mallory?"

The Korting scowled. "Bring her," he said, and several of the dwarves immediately shuffled off. "You would do well to watch what you say. Mulgarath will soon reign over the world, and we, his loyal servants, will be at his side. He will strip the land bare for us and then we will build a glorious new forest of ironwood trees. We will rebuild the world in silver and copper and iron."

Simon crawled to the edge of the cage.

"That doesn't make any sense. What are you going to eat? How are you going to breathe without plants to make oxygen?"

Jared smiled at Simon. Sometimes it wasn't so bad having a know-it-all for a twin brother.

The Korting's scowl deepened. "Do you deny that we dwarves are the greatest crafts-people you have ever seen? You need only to look at my hound there to see our superiority. His silver body is more lovely than any fur, he is faster, he needs no food, and he neither drools nor fawns." The Korting nudged the dog with his foot. The dog turned and stretched before resuming its wheezy sleep.

"I don't think that's what Simon was trying to say," Jared began, but he was interrupted by six dwarves entering the room, a long glass box on their shoulders.

"Mallory!" Jared stared with a sinking feeling in his stomach. The case looked like a coffin.

"What did you do to our sister?" Simon demanded. He looked pale. "She's not dead, is she?"

"Just the opposite," said the dwarf lord with a smile. "She will never die. Look more closely."

The dwarves set down the glass case on an ornately sculpted stand beside Jared and Simon's cage.

Mallory's hair had been arranged and hung in one long braid snaking past her waxy, pale face. A circlet of metal leaves rested above her forehead. Her lips and cheeks were rouged as red as a doll's, yet her hands held the hilt of a silvery blade.

She had been dressed in a white gown of frothy lace. Her eyes were closed, and Jared was almost afraid that if she opened them, they would be made of glass.

"What did they do to her?" said Simon. "It doesn't seem like Mallory at all."

"Her beauty and youth will never fade," said the Korting. "Out of this case she would be doomed to age, death, and decay—the curse of all mortals."

"I think Mallory would rather be doomed," said Jared.

The dwarf lord snorted. "Suit yourself. What have you to give me for her?"

Jared reached into his backpack and brought out the towel-wrapped book. "Arthur Spiderwick's field guide." He felt a twinge of guilt at the lie but ruthlessly quashed it.

The Korting rubbed his hands together. "Excellent. Just as was anticipated. Let's have the book."

"You'll give my sister back to me?"

"She'll be yours."

Jared held out the fake field guide, and one of the dwarves snatched it through the bars. The dwarf lord did not even bother to look at it.

"Take this fine cage to the treasure room, and put the glass case beside it!"

"What?" Jared said. "But you wanted to trade!'"

"We *have* traded," the Korting said with a sneer. "You bargained for your sister, but you never bargained for your freedom."

"No! You can't!" Jared banged his hands on the bars, but it did not keep the dwarves from pushing their moving prison out into a dark corridor. He couldn't look at Simon. After all his yelling at his brother, it was he who was the stupid one, he who hadn't been clever enough. He felt tired and worn-out, small and pathetic. He was just a kid. How was he supposed to find a way out of this?

"You're going to have to feed us."

Chapter Five

IN WHICH Jared and Simon Wake Sleeping Beauty

Jared barely noticed the path they took to the treasure room. He shut his eyes against the burn of tears.

"Here we are," said the dwarf who had brought them. His beard was white, and there was a ring of keys at his hip. He turned to the group carrying the glass box that held Mallory. "Just set that down right there."

The treasure chamber was lit with a single lantern, but the heaps of shining gold reflected the light, so it was not as dim as it might have been. A silver peacock with a lapis-and-coral-studded tail pecked at a copper mouse sitting atop a vase in a way that suggested more boredom than malice.

The white-bearded dwarf peered at them while the others trooped out. He grinned at them fondly. "I'll just see if I can find something for you boys to play with. Perhaps gob stones? They even stand up and hurl themselves."

"I'm hungry," Simon said. "We're not mechanical. If you're going to keep us here, you're going to have to feed us."

The dwarf squinted. "True enough. I'll bring you a mash of spiders and turnips. That will fix you right up."

"How are you going to give it to us?" Jared asked suddenly. "There's no door."

"Oh, there's a door all right," said the dwarf. "I made that cage myself. Sturdy, isn't it?"

"Yeah," said Jared. "Real sturdy." He rolled his eyes. Wasn't it bad enough that they had gotten tricked and were stuck in a *cage*? Did the dwarf really have to rub it in?

"See, the lock is inside this bar." The dwarf tapped one of the bars lightly with his finger. "I had to make the gears really tiny—had to work with a hammer the size of a pin.

If you look, you can see the seam of the door. See? Right there."

"Can you open it?" Simon asked. Jared looked at him with surprise. Had Simon been planning the whole time, while Jared had been busy just being upset?

"You want to see it in action?" asked the dwarf.

"Yeah," Jared said, not quite believing that they were going to get this lucky.

"Well, okay, boys. Now step back for a moment. There. Just once, and then I better get your food. What a treat to finally get to use all of these things."

Jared smiled encouragingly. The dwarf took the key ring from his belt and selected a tiny key. It was the size and shape of a whistle, with a complicated pattern of ridges on it. He inserted it into one of the bars, although Jared

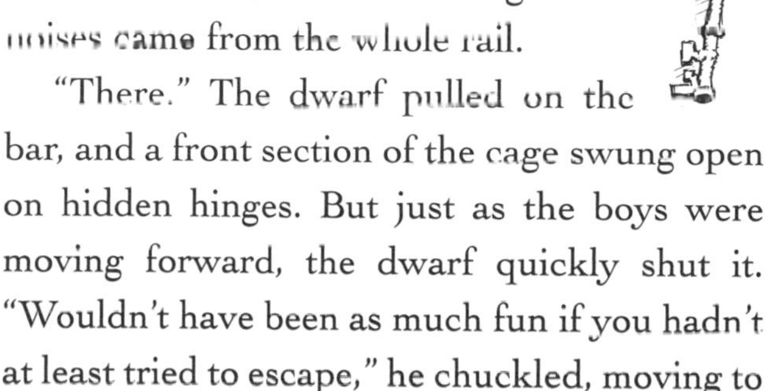

couldn't see the hole from their side of the cage. With a twist of the dwarf's wrist, clicks, clunks, whirrs, and whizzing noises came from the whole rail.

"There." The dwarf pulled on the bar, and a front section of the cage swung open on hidden hinges. But just as the boys were moving forward, the dwarf quickly shut it. "Wouldn't have been as much fun if you hadn't at least tried to escape," he chuckled, moving to hook the key ring back on his belt.

Jared darted his hand out and grabbed for the key ring at the same time. The keys clattered to the floor.

Simon scooped them up before the dwarf could.

"Hey! No fair!" said the dwarf. "Give those back!"

Simon shook his head.

"But you have to. You're prisoners. You can't have the keys."

"We're not giving them back," Jared said.

The dwarf looked panicked. He walked to the edge of the hall and yelled, "Quick—someone! Send guards! The prisoners are escaping!" When no one came, he fixed Jared and Simon with a glare. "You'd better stay right there," he said, and darted out into the hall, still calling for guards.

Simon fitted the key into the door, and they jumped out of the cage. "Hurry, they're coming!"

"We have to get Mallory!" Jared gestured to her case.

"There's no time," said Simon. "We'll come back."

"Wait," Jared said. "Let's hide here! They'll think we ran away."

Simon looked panicked. "Where?"

"On top of the cage!" Jared pointed to the solid silver lid of the cage. He scrambled on top of a nearby pile of loot and used it to climb up. "Come on!"

Simon climbed halfway, and Jared hauled him onto the top. They had just enough time to curl up tightly before dwarves burst into the room.

"They're not here, either," one dwarf said. "Not in the hallway, not in any of the nearby rooms."

Jared smirked against the cool metal.

"Wind up the dogs. They'll find them."

"Dogs?" Simon mouthed to Jared as the dwarves shuffled out of the room.

"What's the matter?" Jared smiled, giddy at the success of their plan. "You love dogs."

Simon rolled his eyes and dropped to the

"They're not here, either."

floor, kicking a candelabrum and scattering a few pieces of hematite. He picked up one and tucked it in his pocket.

"Stop making so much noise," Jared said, trying to climb down carefully and nearly toppling a copper rosebush.

They knelt beside the glass case, and Jared unlatched it. There was a hiss as the lid lifted, as though some invisible gas was escaping. Inside, Mallory was motionless.

"Mallory," Jared said. "Get up." He pulled at her arm, but it was limp and flopped back onto her chest when he let go.

"You don't think someone needs to kiss her, do you?" Simon asked. "Like Snow White?"

"That's gross." Jared couldn't remember anything about kissing in the field guide, but he couldn't remember anything about glass coffins, either. He leaned in and gave her a quick peck on the cheek. There was no response.

"We have to do something," Simon said. "We don't have much time."

Jared grabbed a lock of Mallory's hair and tugged hard. She twitched slightly and half opened her eyes. Jared sighed with relief.

"Getoffme," she muttered, and tried to turn on her side.

"Help me get her up," Jared said, moving the sword off her and onto the floor.

He pulled her body a little ways up before she slipped back into the case.

"Come on, Mal," Jared said into her ear. *"Up!"*

Simon slapped her cheek. She twitched again, opening her eyes groggily.

"Wha—," she managed.

"You have to get out of there," said Simon. "Stand up."

"Lean on the sword like a cane," Jared suggested.

With her brothers' help Mallory managed to get on her feet and stagger out into the hallway. It was empty.

"Lean on the sword like a cane."

"For once," Simon said, "things are actually going our way."

Just then they heard the distant sound of hollow, metallic barking.

"The stones. The stones speak. They speak to me."

Chapter Six

IN WHICH the Stones Speak

Jared and Simon ran, half dragging Mallory, through a series of hallways and narrow, dim rooms. Once, they passed through an overhang high above a central cavity where the Korting oversaw dwarves laboring to stack weapons onto carts. The barking, at first far off, became closer and more frenzied. They continued on, through chamber after chamber, ducking behind stalagmites when they heard dwarves nearby, and then creeping on.

Jared stopped in a cavern with pools where white, sightless fish darted. Tiny rocks were balanced atop the points of all the stalagmites, and the sound of water droplets echoed through the space, along with a strange tapping rhythm.

"Where are we?"

"I'm not sure," Simon said. "I would have remembered those fish, but I don't. I don't think we came this way when they brought us in."

"Where are we?" Mallory moaned, swaying slightly as she stood.

"We can't go back," Jared said nervously. "We have to keep going."

A small, pale figure jumped out from the shadows. It had huge, luminous eyes that shone in the gloom. On its forehead, two long whiskers quivered.

"Wha—what's that?" Simon whispered.

The creature tapped on the wall with one long, multijointed finger, then pressed a large ear against the stone. Jared noticed that the creature's nails were cracked and broken.

"Thestones. Thestonesspeak. Theyspeaktome." It had a small, whispery voice, and Jared strained to pick out individual words. The creature tapped again. The sound was like some demented Morse code.

"Hey," Jared said. "Um, do you know the way out of here?"

"Shhhhh." It closed its eyes and nodded its head in time with something Jared couldn't hear. Then it leaped into Jared's arms, wrapping

a strong hand around his neck. Jared stumbled backward.

"Yes! Yes! Thestonessaytocrawlthroughthere." It pointed into the darkness, past the pools of white fish.

"Um, great. Thanks." Jared tried to peel the creature off. Finally it unlatched, scrambled to the wall, and began tapping again.

"What is that?" Simon whispered to Jared. "A really weird dwarf?"

"A nodder or a banger, I think," Jared whispered back. "They live in mines and warn miners of collapses and stuff."

Simon made a face. "Are they all insane? It's worse than that phooka."

"Foryou,JaredGrace." The creature pressed a smooth, cold stone into Jared's hand. *"Thestonewantstotravelwithyou."*

"Uh, thanks," Jared said. "We have to go

"The stones speak."

now." He moved toward the dark place that the nodder-banger-thing had indicated. As Jared got closer, he thought he could make out a crevice.

"Wait. How did you know Jared's name?" Mallory asked, moving slowly behind her brothers.

Jared turned back, suddenly confused. "Yeah, how *did* you know my name?" he demanded.

The creature rapped on the cave wall again, an uneven series of taps. *"Thestonestellme. Thestonesknowall."*

"Riiiight." Jared continued on. The creature had actually pointed them toward a small opening in the wall of the cave. They had overlooked it before. The hole was low to the ground and very dark. Jared got on his hands and knees and started to crawl. The cave floor was moist, and sometimes he thought he could hear a slither or a rustle just ahead of him. His brother and sister shuffled along behind. Once or twice he heard one of them gasp, but he didn't slow his pace. He could still hear the barking of the dogs echoing through the caverns.

They emerged in the hall of the ironwood tree.

"I think it's that way," Jared said, pointing to one of the hallways.

They ran down the path until they came to a long fissure, almost as wide as Jared was tall. He looked down into the darkness. It was as black as if the crack went on forever.

"We have to jump!" Simon said. "Come on!"

"What?" said Mallory.

The barking was close behind them. Jared

Together they leaped.

saw red eyes in the gloom. Simon stepped back, then sprung across, landing hard.

"You have to!" Jared said, and grabbed hold of his sister's hand. Together they leaped. Mallory stumbled when her foot hit the rock on the other side, but she fell safely onto the cave floor. They sprinted off, hoping the dogs could not jump as far as they had.

But this passage circled around, and they found themselves back in the central hall, massive branches hanging above them, metal birds twittering.

"Where are we going?" Mallory whined as she leaned on the sword.

"I don't know," Jared said, catching his breath. "I don't know! I don't know!"

"I think maybe that way," Simon offered.

"We already went that way, and we wound up here!" The barking of the dogs was so close that Jared expected them to burst into the room at any moment.

"How can you not know where to go?" Mallory demanded. "Do you remember how you got in here?"

"I'm trying! It was dark, and we were in a cage! What do you want me to do?" Jared kicked the base of the tree as if to emphasize his point.

The leaves quivered, clanging together like a thousand chimes. The sound was deafening. One of the copper birds fell to the ground, its wings still twitching and its beak opening and closing soundlessly.

"Oh, crap," said Mallory.

Metal dogs burst into the room from several corridors, their sleek, jointed bodies effortlessly covering the distance between the entrance and the siblings. Their garnet eyes blazed.

"Climb!" Jared yelled, hooking his foot on

Metal dogs burst into the room.

the lowest branch and reaching back for his sister's hand. Simon clamored up the rough iron bark. Mallory lifted herself dazedly.

"Come on, Mallory!" Simon pleaded.

She swung her leg onto a branch just as a dog lunged. Its teeth caught hold of the end of her white dress and ripped it. The other dogs swarmed close, tearing the cloth.

Jared threw the stone that he'd been clutching in one hand. It flew past the dog's head and rolled ineffectually against the cave wall.

One of the dogs bounded after the rock. At first Jared thought that maybe the stone was magical. Then he noticed that the dog had carried it back in its teeth, metal tail wagging like a whip.

"Simon," Jared said. "I think that dog is *playing*."

Simon looked at the dog for a moment and then started to shimmy down the tree.

"What are you doing?" Mallory demanded. "Mechanical robot dogs are not pets!"

"Don't worry," Simon called back.

Simon dropped to the ground, and the dogs stopped barking suddenly, nosing him as though

deciding whether or not to bite. Simon stood very still. Watching him, Jared couldn't breathe.

"Good boys," Simon soothed, his voice shaking only slightly. "Want to fetch? Want to play a game?" He reached forward and gingerly took the stone from between the dog's metal teeth.

All the dogs bounced in the air at once, barking happily. Simon looked up at his siblings and smiled.

"You have got to be kidding me," Mallory said.

Simon threw the stone, and all five dogs bounded after it. One snatched it up in its jaws and marched back proudly, the others trailing eagerly. Simon leaned down to pet their metal heads. Their silver tongues lolled from their mouths.

Simon threw the rock three more times before Jared called down to him.

"We have to go," he said. "The dwarves are

going to find us if we wait any longer."

Simon looked disappointed. "Okay," he shouted to them. Then he took the stone and hurled it as hard as he could into the other room. The dogs thundered after it. "Come on!"

Jared and Mallory jumped down. All three of them ran to the small crack in the wall and squeezed inside, crawling rapidly on their hands and knees. Jared stuffed his backpack behind him, blocking the way. Already he could hear the dogs whining and scratching at the cloth.

They felt their way in the dark, but there must have been a fork in the tunnel that they'd missed earlier, because this time there was a soft, warm light at the end of the corridor.

They found themselves standing above the quarry on dewy grass. Dawn reddened the sky in the east.

"What happened?"

Chapter Seven

IN WHICH There Is an Unexpected Betrayal

Mallory looked down at herself in disgust. "I *hate* dresses. What happened? Why did I wake up in a glass box?"

Jared shook his head. "We're not really sure—I guess the dwarves grabbed you somehow. Do you remember anything?"

"I was packing up my things after the match." She shrugged. "Some kid said that you were in trouble."

"Shhh," Simon said, pointing into the quarry. "Get down."

They knelt in the grass and peered over the

edge. A horde of goblins poured out of the caves. They skittered and rolled, gnashing their teeth and barking before fanning out and sniffing the air. Behind them was a massive monster with dead branches for hair. It wore the dark, tattered remains of clothes from another time, and big, curving horns rose up from his brow.

From the cave entrance the Korting and his dwarven courtiers appeared. Behind them came more goblins, who were pulling a cart filled with shining weapons. With that last group a prisoner stumbled along ahead of them. The prisoner was the size of an adult human, a sack covering the person's head, both wrists and ankles bound with dirty cloth. Something about the person seemed familiar. The goblins pushed the prisoner out into

the quarry, poking the figure with sharp sticks, far from where the monster stood.

"Who is that?" Mallory whispered, squinting.

"I can't see," said Jared. "Why would they need a prisoner?"

The Korting cleared his throat nervously as a hush fell over the crowd. "Great Lord Mulgarath, we thank you for the honor of allowing us to serve you."

Mulgarath stopped. The ogre's great horned head loomed over the rest of the creatures as he turned back to the dwarves with a sneer.

Jared swallowed hard. *Mulgarath.* The word had never meant much to him before, but now he was afraid. Even though he knew the monster couldn't see him, he felt those dark eyes sweep over the throng and wanted to duck down lower.

"Are these all the weapons I asked for?" Mulgarath's ringing tones echoed through the quarry. He pointed to the cart.

"Yes, of course," said the dwarf lord. "A show of our loyalty, our dedication to your new regime. You will find no finer blades, no better craftsmanship. I would stake my life on it!"

"Would you?" asked the ogre. He drew Jared's fake field guide from a large pocket. "And this—would you also stake your life that this is the book I asked you to obtain?"

The dwarf lord hesitated. "I . . . I did as you asked. . . ."

The ogre held up a battered book with a laugh. Jared realized it was the same laugh that the Not-Jared had made in the hallway at school.

Jared gasped and Mallory elbowed him hard.

"You have been duped, dwarf lord. No matter. I have Arthur Spiderwick's Guide," Mulgarath said. "The final thing I need to begin my reign."

The dwarf bowed low. "You are great indeed," the Korting said. "A worthy master."

"I may be a worthy master, but I am not at all sure that you make worthy servants." He

"Kill them!"

raised his hand, and his goblins stopped their scuffling and scrabbling. "Kill them!"

It happened so fast that Jared couldn't follow it all. The goblins seemed to surge forth as one, some stopping to pick up the dwarf-forged weapons, most just attacking with their claws and teeth. The dwarves hesitated, shouting, and that moment of panic and confusion was enough for the goblins to be upon them.

The goblins bit, clawed, and slashed until not a single dwarf was left standing.

Jared felt sick and numb. He had never seen anything be killed before. Looking down, he felt like he might throw up. "We have to stop them."

"There's no way we can do this alone. Look at them all," Mallory said. Jared glanced at the sword still clutched in Mallory's hand, its fine blade gleaming in the rising sun. It would

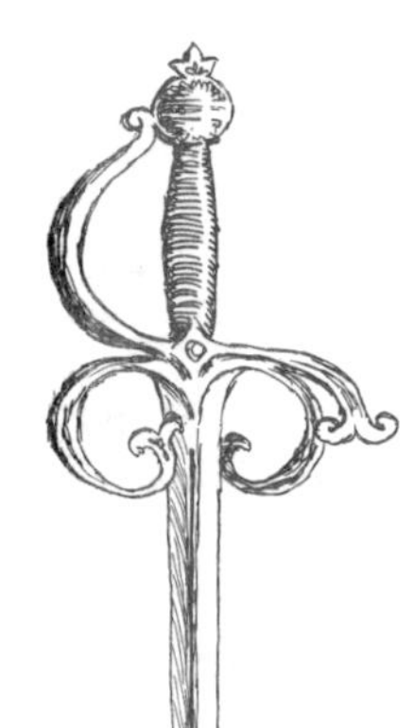

never be enough to take on all of them.

"We *have* to tell Mom what's going on," Simon said.

"She won't believe us!" Jared said. He wiped the wetness from his eyes with his shirt sleeve and tried not to look down at the broken bodies in the quarry. "What if she doesn't believe us?"

"We have to try," said Mallory.

And so, with the screams of dwarves still echoing in their ears, the three Grace children started toward home.

End of
BOOK FOUR

About TONY DiTERLIZZI . . .

A *New York Times* best-selling author, Tony DiTerlizzi created the Zena Sutherland Award–winning *Ted, Jimmy Zangwow's Out-of-This-World Moon Pie Adventure,* as well as illustrations in Tony Johnston's Alien and Possum beginning-reader series. Most recently, his brilliantly cinematic version of Mary Howitt's classic *The Spider and the Fly* was awarded a Caldecott Honor. In addition, Tony's art has graced the work of such well-known fantasy names as J.R.R. Tolkien, Anne McCaffrey, Peter S. Beagle, and Greg Bear as well as Wizards of the Coast's *Magic The Gathering*. He and his wife, Angela, reside with their pug, Goblin, in Amherst, Massachusetts. Visit Tony on the World Wide Web at www.diterlizzi.com.

and HOLLY BLACK

An avid collector of rare folklore volumes, Holly Black spent her early years in a decaying Victorian mansion where her mother fed her a steady diet of ghost stories and books about faeries. Accordingly, her first novel, *Tithe: A Modern Faerie Tale,* is a gothic and artful glimpse at the world of Faerie. Published in the fall of 2002, it received two starred reviews and a Best Book for Young Adults citation from the American Library Association. She lives in West Long Branch, New Jersey, with her husband, Theo, and a remarkable menagerie. Visit Holly on the World Wide Web at www.blackholly.com.

Tony and Holly continue to work day and night fending off angry faeries and goblins in order to bring the Grace children's story to you.

Who has been captured?
Is the Guide gone?
Can three weary children
do it alone?

Can they face an ogre
with an evil plan
to conquer the planet
and poison the land?

Or is there someone
brave, strong, and wise
who can battle a monster
and come out alive?

Where is our hero?
Seek Spiderwick five.

ACKNOWLEDGMENTS

Tony and Holly would like to thank
Steve and Dianna for their insight,
Starr for her honesty,
Josh and Lisa for their attention to detail,
Myles and Liza for sharing the journey,
Ellen and Julie for helping make this our reality,
Kevin for his tireless enthusiasm and faith in us,
and especially Angela and Theo —
there are not enough superlatives
to describe your patience
in enduring endless nights
of Spiderwick discussion.

The text type for this book is set in Cochin.
The display types are set in Nevins Hand and Rackham.
The illustrations are rendered in pen and ink.
Production editor: Dorothy Gribbin
Art director: Dan Potash
Production managers: Chava Wolin and Karene Petrillo

The dragon coiled around Byron.

Tony DiTerlizzi *and* Holly Black

Simon and Schuster Books for Young Readers
New York London Toronto Sydney

SIMON & SCHUSTER BOOKS FOR YOUNG READERS
An imprint of Simon & Schuster Children's Publishing Division
1230 Avenue of the Americas, New York, New York 10020

 • Book design by Tony DiTerlizzi and Dan Potash • Manufactured in the United States of America

12 14 16 18 20 19 17 15 13 11

CIP data for this book is available from the Library of Congress.
ISBN 0-689-85940-6

For my grandmother, Melvina,
who said I should write a book just like this one
and to whom I replied that I never would
—H. B.

For Arthur Rackham,
may you continue to inspire others
as you have me
—T. D.

Table of
Contents

List of Full-Page
Illustrations

Dear Reader,

Over the years that Tony and I have been friends, we've shared the same childhood fascination with faeries. We did not realize the importance of that bond or how it might be tested.

One day Tony and I—along with several other authors—were doing a signing at a large bookstore. When the signing was over, we lingered, helping to stack books and chatting, until a clerk approached us. He said that there had been a letter left for us. When I inquired which one of us, we were surprised by his answer.

"Both of you," he said.

The letter was exactly as reproduced on the following page. Tony spent a long time just staring at the photocopy that came with it. Then, in a hushed voice, he wondered aloud about the remainder of the manuscript. We hurriedly wrote a note, tucked it back into the envelope, and asked the clerk to deliver it to the Grace children.

Not long after, a package arrived on my doorstep, bound in red ribbon. A few days after that, three children rang the bell and told me this story.

What has happened since is hard to describe. Tony and I have been plunged into a world we never quite believed in. We now see that faeries are far more than childhood stories. There is an invisible world around us and we hope that you, dear reader, will open your eyes to it.

HOLLY BLACK

Dear Mrs. Black and Mr. DiTerlizzi:

I know that a lot of people don't believe in faeries, but I do and I think that you do too. After I read your books, I told my brothers about you and we decided to write. We know about real faeries. In fact, we know a lot about them.

The page attached* to this one is a photocopy from an old book we found in our attic. It isn't a great copy because we had some trouble with the copier. The book tells people how to identify faeries and how to protect themselves. Can you please give this book to your publisher? If you can, please put a letter in this envelope and give it back to the store. We will find a way to send the book. The normal mail is too dangerous.

We just want people to know about this. The stuff that has happened to us could happen to anyone.

Sincerely,

Mallory, Jared, and Simon Grace

*Not included.

The Junkyard
The Camp
The Bridge
The Spiderwick Estate
Rountree Street
Dulac Drive
The Grove

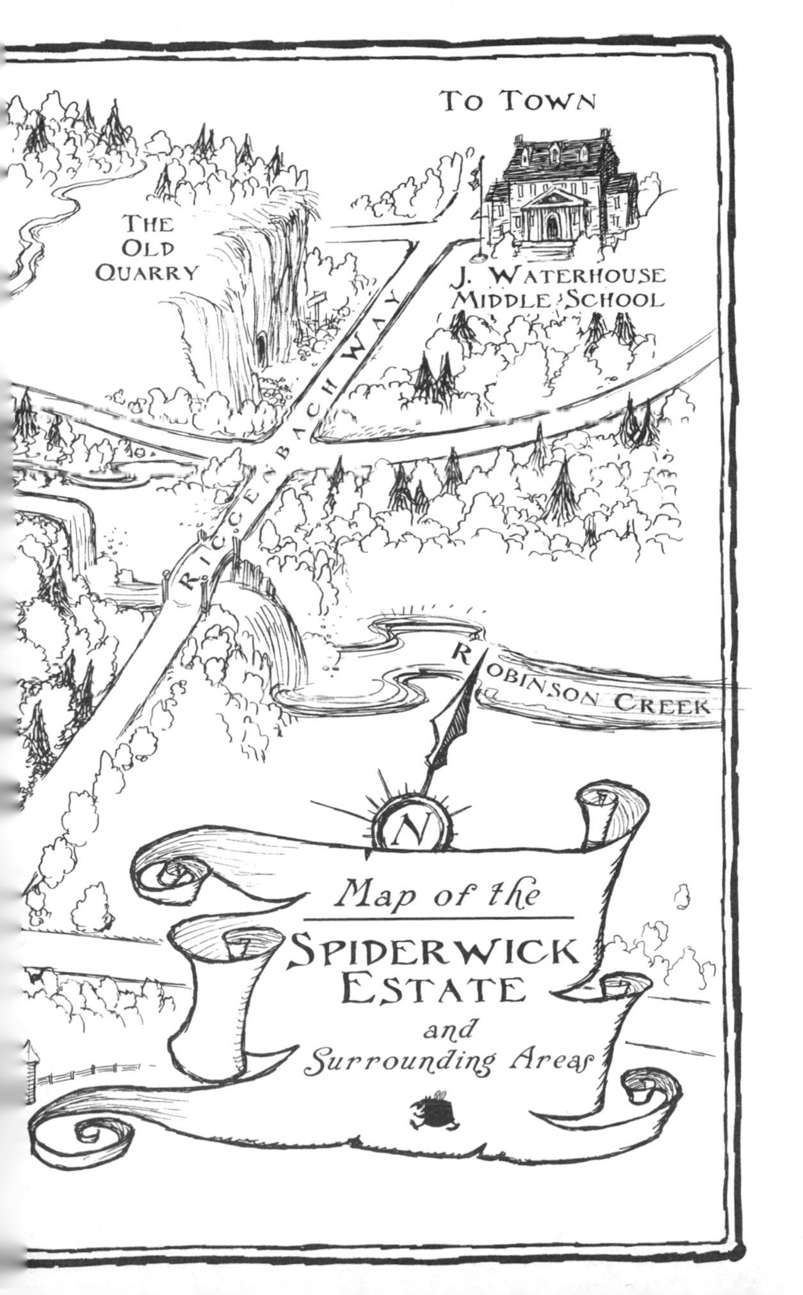

To Town
The Old Quarry
J. Waterhouse Middle School
Riccebach Way
Robinson Creek
N
Map of the
Spiderwick Estate
and
Surrounding Areas

THE SPIDERWICK CHRONICLES

At the gate of the Spiderwick estate

Chapter One

IN WHICH the World Is Turned Upside Down

The pale light of the newly risen sun made the dew shimmer on the nearby grass as Jared, Mallory, and Simon trudged along the early morning roads. They were tired, but the need to get home kept them going. Mallory shivered in her thin white dress, clutching her sword so hard that her knuckles went white. Beside her, Simon shuffled along, kicking stray bits of asphalt. Jared was quiet too. Each time his eyes closed, even for a moment, all he saw were goblins—hundreds of goblins, with Mulgarath at their head.

Jared tried to distract himself by planning what he would say to his mother when they finally got home. She was going to be furious with them for being gone all night and even madder at Jared because of that thing with the knife. But he could explain everything now. He imagined telling her about the shape-shifting ogre, the rescue of Mallory from the dwarves, and the way they had tricked the elves. His mother would look at the sword and she would have to believe them. And then she would forgive Jared for everything.

A sharp sound, like a tea kettle whistling at full volume, snapped him back to the present. They were at the gate of the Spiderwick estate. To Jared's horror, trash, papers, feathers, and broken furniture littered the lawn.

"What is all that?" Mallory gasped.

A screech drew Jared's eyes upward, where

Simon's griffin was chasing a small creature around the roof and knocking pieces of slate loose. Stray feathers drifted over the roof tiles.

"Byron!" Simon called, but the griffin either didn't hear or chose to ignore him. Simon turned to Jared in exasperation. "He shouldn't be up there. His wing is still hurt."

"What's he after?" Mallory asked, squinting.

"A goblin, I think," said Jared slowly. The memory of teeth and claws red with blood awakened a horrible dread within him.

"Mom!" Mallory gasped, and began to run toward the house.

Jared and Simon raced after her. Up close they could see that the windows of the old estate were smashed and the front door hung by a single hinge.

They darted inside, through the mudroom, stepping over scattered keys and torn coats. In the kitchen, water poured from the faucet, filling a sink piled with broken plates and spilling onto the floor, where food from the overturned freezer was defrosting in wet piles. The wallboard had been punched open in places, and plaster dust, mingling with spilled flour and cereal, covered the stove.

The dining room table was still upright, but several of the chairs were knocked over, their caning ripped. One of their great-uncle's paintings was slashed and the frame was cracked, although it still hung on the wall.

The living room was worse: The television was shattered and their game console had been shoved through it. The sofas were ripped open, and stuffing was scattered across the floorboards like drifts of snow. And there, sitting on the remains of a brocade footstool, was Thimbletack.

"All my fault, all my fault."

As Jared moved closer to the little brownie, he could see that Thimbletack had a long, raw scratch on his shoulder and that his hat was missing. He blinked up at Jared with wet, black eyes.

"All my fault, all my fault," Thimbletack said. "I tried to fight; my magic's too slight." A tear rolled down his thin cheek, and he wiped it away angrily. "Goblins alone I might have driven off. The ogre just looked at me and scoffed."

"Where's Mom?" Jared demanded. He could feel himself trembling.

"Just before the break of day, they bound her and carried her away," Thimbletack said.

"They *can't* have!" Simon's voice was close to a squeak. "Mom!" he called, rushing to the stairs and shouting up to the next landing. *"Mom!"*

"We have to do something," said Mallory.

"We *saw* her," Jared said softly, sitting down on the ruined couch. He felt light-headed, and hot and cold at the same time. "At the quarry. She was the adult the goblins had with them. Mulgarath had her, and we didn't even notice. We should have listened—*I* should have listened. I never should have opened Uncle Arthur's stupid book."

The brownie shook his head vigorously. "To protect the house and those inside is *my* duty, Guide or no Guide."

"But if I had destroyed it like you said, none of this would have happened!" Jared punched himself in the leg.

Thimbletack scrubbed his eyes with the heel of

his hand. "No one knows if that is true or not. I hid it away—see what we got?"

"Enough with the pity party—neither of you is helping!" Mallory squatted beside the footstool, handing the brownie his hat. "Where would they have taken Mom?"

Thimbletack shook his head sadly. "Goblins are filthy things, the master worse than his hirelings. They would dwell somewhere as foul as they, but where that is, I cannot say."

From above them there was a whistle and a clatter.

"One goblin is still on the roof," said Simon, looking up. "It must know!"

Jared stood up. "We'd better stop Byron before he eats it."

"Right," said Simon, heading up the stairs.

The three kids ran up the steps and down the hall toward the attic. The bedroom doors on the second floor were open. Torn clothing, pillow feathers, and ripped bedding spilled out into the hall. Outside Jared and Simon's shared room, cracked, empty tanks lay on the floor. Simon froze, a stricken expression on his face.

"Lemondrop?" Simon called. "Jeffrey? Kitty?"

"Come on," Jared said. As he steered Simon away from the wreckage of their room, he caught sight of the hall closet. The shelves were dripping with lotions and shampoos, which had also soaked the scattered towels. And at the bottom, near deep scratches in the wallboard, the secret door to Arthur's library had been ripped off its hinges.

"How did they find it?" Mallory asked.

Simon shook his head. "I guess they ransacked the place looking for it."

Jared crouched down and wriggled into

Arthur Spiderwick's library. Bright sunlight streaming through the single window showed the damage clearly. Tears burned his eyes as he stepped across a carpet of shredded pages. Arthur's books had been ripped free of their bindings and scattered. Torn sketches and toppled bookshelves littered the floor. Jared looked around the room helplessly.

"Well?" Mallory called.

"Destroyed," Jared said. "Everything's destroyed."

"Come on," Simon called. "We have to get that goblin."

Jared nodded his head, despite the fact that neither his brother nor his sister could see him, and moved numbly toward the door. There was something about the desecration of this one room—a room that had remained secret all these years—that made Jared feel as

"Everything's destroyed."

though nothing would ever be right again.

Together he, Simon, and Mallory trudged up the stairs to the attic, crossing over glittering pieces of smashed holiday ornaments and stepping past a broken dress form. In the dim light Jared could see dust erupting in time with the clattering of griffin claws, and he could hear more screeching above them.

"One more level and we can step right onto the roof," Jared said, pointing to the final staircase. It led to the single highest room in the house, a small tower with half-boarded windows on all four sides.

"I think I heard some barking," Simon said as they climbed. "That goblin must still be okay."

When they reached the top of the tower, Mallory swung her sword at the window boards, splintering them. Jared tried to pry off what was left loose.

"I'll go first," Simon said, hopping onto the ledge and gingerly climbing past the jagged slats and onto the roof.

"Wait!" Jared shouted. "What makes you think you can control that griffin?" But Simon didn't seem to be paying attention.

Mallory strapped on a belt, wrapping it around the sword so it hung from her hip. "Come on!"

Jared swung his legs over the sill and stepped out onto the slate. The sudden sunlight almost blinded him, and for a moment his blurry eyes scanned the forest beyond their lawn.

Then he saw Simon approaching the griffin, who had cornered the goblin against one of the brick chimneys. The goblin was Hogsqueal.

"Stop gawping, snail-heads!"

Chapter Two

IN WHICH an Old Friend Returns

"Stop gawping, snail-heads!" Hogsqueal yelled. "Help me!" He was backed against a chimney, one hand holding his coat closed over a largish object, the other brandishing an empty slingshot menacingly.

"Hogsqueal?" Jared grinned at the sight of the hobgoblin, then stopped with a scowl. "What are you doing here?"

Simon was holding the griffin back, mostly by standing between him and Hogsqueal and yelling loudly. Byron turned his hawk head to the side and blinked, then pawed the ground with his talons as though he were more feline than bird. Jared suspected that Byron thought they were playing a new game.

Hogsqueal hesitated, seeing Jared's face. "I didn't know this was *your* house until the griffin showed up."

"You helped catch our mother?" Jared could feel his face growing warm. "Trash our house? Kill Simon's pets?" He took two steps toward Hogsqueal, hands fisting. He'd *trusted* Hogsqueal. He'd *liked* him. And the hobgoblin had *betrayed* them. Jared could barely think with the roaring in his ears.

"I didn't kill anything." Hogsqueal opened his coat a little, revealing a marmalade ball of fur.

"Kitty!" Simon said, distracted by the sight of the kitten.

In that moment Byron lunged past Simon,

catching the hobgoblin's arm in his beak.

"Aaaaaaahhhhh!" Hogsqueal screamed. The cat yowled, jumping onto the roof.

"Byron, no!" Simon yelled. "Drop him!"

The griffin shook his head, whipping Hogsqueal back and forth. The hobgoblin's shouts became louder.

"Do something!" Jared called, panicked.

Simon stepped up to the griffin and hit him hard on the beak with his hand. "NO!" he shouted.

"Oh crap, don't do *that*!" Mallory said, reaching for the sword at her waist. But instead of attacking, the griffin stopped shaking Hogsqueal and looked at Simon with something like alarm.

"Drop him!" Simon repeated, pointing to the slate roof.

Hogsqueal struggled ineffectually, pushing

"I'm sorry, gobstoppers."

his fingers into Byron's nose slits and trying to bite the feathery neck with his baby teeth. The griffin ignored the hobgoblin but didn't make a move to put him down either.

"Be careful," Jared told his brother. "Better he eats Hogsqueal than us."

"Noooo! I'm sorry, gobstoppers," Hogsqueal said, still writhing. "I didn't mean it! Honest. Get me out of here! Heeeeeelp!"

"Jared," Simon said. "Grab Hogsqueal, okay?"

Jared nodded, edging nearer. This close, he could smell the griffin—it had a feral scent, like a cat's fur.

Simon put one hand on the top of Byron's beak, the other on the bottom, and started to lever them apart, repeating, "Be a gooooood boy. Yes. Drop the goblin."

"*Hob*goblin!" Hogsqueal yelped.

"Are you crazy?" Mallory hollered at her brother. The griffin turned his head abruptly in her direction, almost knocking Simon sprawling.

"Sorry," Mallory said in a much smaller voice.

Jared gripped Hogsqueal around the legs. "Got him."

"Hey, yaffner, we're not going to be playing tug-of-war with my body, right? Right?"

Jared just smiled grimly.

Simon tried again to push Byron's beak open. "Mallory, come and help me. Grab the bottom of the beak, and I'll get the top."

She stepped carefully across the slanted roof. The griffin eyed her nervously.

"When I say pull," Simon said, *"pull."*

Together they tried to pry the griffin's jaws apart. Mallory's fingers slid into Byron's mouth as she strained, nearly hanging from the griffin, trying to use her weight against him. Byron struggled and then suddenly gave in, opening his mouth and dropping Hogsqueal's full weight into Jared's arms. Losing his balance, Jared slid backward on the shingles, letting go of Hogsqueal and scrabbling for a handhold. The hobgoblin slid as well, knocking loose the shingle Jared was gripping on to. Jared slipped and grabbed hold of the gutter moments before he would have fallen off the side of the house.

Simon and Mallory looked at Jared with wide eyes. He swallowed hard. As they moved to haul him back onto the roof, Jared saw Hogsqueal make for the open window.

"He's getting away!" Jared said, trying to pull himself higher. His elbow dug into the dried leaves and mud that clotted the gutter.

"Forget about the stupid goblin," Mallory said. "Grab hold of me."

They hauled him back onto the roof. As soon as he was upright, Jared ran after Hogsqueal with Mallory and Simon close behind. They thundered down the stairs.

Hogsqueal was sprawled in the hall outside their bedrooms, and yellow yarn was wrapping itself around him. Jared gaped as the yarn tied itself in a bow.

Thimbletack hopped up on Hogsqueal's head. "I will help you fight the fey. I believe I've a debt to pay."

Jared looked at the yarn and then back at Thimbletack. "I didn't know you could do that!" He remembered how his shoelaces had seemed to tie themselves together and suddenly had an explanation.

The little brownie grinned. "Being unseen

"He's getting away!"

is not enough to get things clean."

"Hey," Hogsqueal yelled. "Get this crazy kipper off me! I wasn't running out on you. I was escaping from that tooby monster on the roof!"

"Shut up," Mallory said.

"That goblin is not misunderstood," said Thimbletack. "He is just plain no good."

"That noddy brownie's a fine one to talk," said Hogsqueal.

"You're going to tell us everything you know, or we're going to spread ketchup on you and put you right back up on the roof," said Jared. Right then he

was so angry that he meant every word of it.

Thimbletack jumped down onto the leg of an overturned coffee table. "That would be overly kind to a goblin in a bind. No, we'll set rats to nibble off your toes, poke out your eyes, and put them up your nose. Your fingers we'll remove with dull scissors, and we'll wait until your confidence withers."

Simon paled but said nothing.

Hogsqueal squirmed in his bindings. "I'll tell you already, surly-boots. No need to threaten!"

"Where is our mom?" Jared demanded. "Where would they have taken her?"

"Mulgarath's lair is at the dump on the edge of town. He's built a palace of trash, and it's defended by his goblin army and by other things besides. Don't be a pumpkin-head.

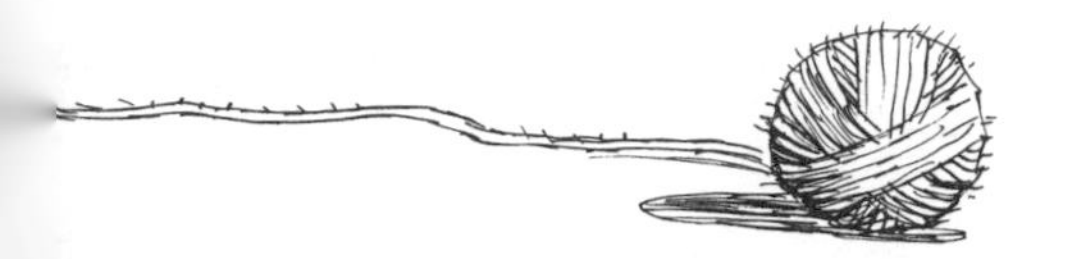

There is no way you can get in there."

"What other things are defending it?" Jared demanded.

"Dragons," Hogsqueal said. "Little ones, mostly."

"Dragons?" Jared repeated in horror. Arthur's field guide had notes on dragons, but Arthur himself had never seen one. All of his accounts were secondhand. But even secondhand, the stories were frightening—they described poisonous venom, teeth as sharp as daggers, and bodies that were as quick as whips.

"And you were part of Mulgarath's goblin army?" Mallory asked, eyes narrowed.

"I had to be!" Hogsqueal exclaimed. "Everyone was joining up! Where was I supposed to go, chatter-basket?"

"What did you tell them happened to the

other goblins—the ones you were with before?"

"*Other* goblins?" Hogsqueal said. "For the last time, lily-pants, I'm a *hob*goblin! You might as well call a blackbird a crow!"

Jared sighed. "So, what *did* you say?"

Hogsqueal rolled his eyes. "What do you think, beetle-guts? I said a troll ate 'em, simple as that."

"If we untie you, will you take us to the dump?" Mallory demanded.

"Probably too late." Hogsqueal grunted.

"What was that?" Jared scowled.

"Yes," Hogsqueal said. "*Yes!* I'll take you. Are you happy, snotters? Just as long as I don't have to see that griffin again."

"But, Jared," Simon said, a small smile twisting his mouth, "it would be a lot faster if we flew."

"Wait, now! I didn't agree to that!" Hogsqueal exclaimed.

"We need a plan," Mallory said, stepping away from the hobgoblin and lowering her voice. "How can we beat an army of goblins, a dragon, and a shape-shifting ogre?"

"There has to be something," said Jared, following her. "They must have a weakness." The pages of Arthur's Guide that had once been so clear in his mind had faded, his memory growing increasingly spotty. He tried to concentrate, to remember anything that might be important.

"Too bad we don't have the field guide." Simon stared at the broken fish tanks as though some answer could be found among the glass shards.

"But we know where Arthur is," said Jared carefully, a plan starting to form in his mind. "We could ask him."

"Just how are you suggesting we do that?" Mallory asked, one hand on her hip.

"I'm going to ask the elves to let me talk to him." Jared spoke as though that were a perfectly reasonable suggestion.

Mallory's eyes widened with surprise. "The last time we saw the elves, they weren't exactly what I would call *friendly.*"

"Yeah, they wanted to trap me underground forever," said Simon.

"You have to trust me," Jared said slowly. "I can do it. They promised that they wouldn't hold me there against my will ever again."

"I trust *you,*" said Mallory. "It's the elves I don't trust, and you shouldn't either. I'm going to come."

Jared shook his head. "There isn't enough time. Get Hogsqueal to tell you everything he knows about Mulgarath. I'll be back as soon as I can." He looked down at the little brownie. "I'll bring Thimbletack—if he'll come."

"I thought it had to be just you," said Simon.

"I have to be the only human," Jared said, his eyes still fixed on Thimbletack.

"I have not been out of the house in years." With that, Thimbletack walked to the edge of the chair and let Jared put him into the hood

of Jared's sweatshirt. "But I must put aside my fears."

They left before Simon or Mallory could talk them out of it. Crossing the street, they started up the hill toward the elven grove. The late-morning sky had deepened to a bright, cloudless blue, and Jared hurried, afraid that they didn't have much time.

"It is true I took the book."

Chapter Three

IN WHICH Jared Finds Out Things He Doesn't Want to Know

The grove was the same as he remembered it—tree-rimmed with mushrooms in the center—but this time when Jared stepped into the middle, nothing happened. No branches laced together to trap him, no roots wound around his ankles, and no elves appeared to scold him.

"Hello!" Jared yelled. He waited a moment, but the only reply was the distant calling of birds.

Frustrated, Jared paced back and forth. "Is

anyone here? I'm kind of in a hurry!"

Still nothing. Minutes passed.

Looking at the ring of mushrooms, he had an overwhelming urge to strike out at the elves. If only they hadn't taken Arthur.

He'd just lifted his foot to kick one when he heard a soft voice from the tree line.

"Reckless child, what are you doing in this place?" It was the green-eyed female elf, her hair tinged with more reds and browns than it had been before. And her gown was now deep amber and gold, like summer giving way to fall. Her voice sounded more sad than angry.

"Please," Jared said. "Mulgarath has my mother. I have to save her. You have to let me talk to Arthur."

"What should I care for one mortal?" She turned toward the trees. "Do you know how many of my own people have been lost? How many dwarves—old as the stones beneath our feet—are no more?"

"I saw it," Jared said. "We were there. Please—I'll give you anything. I'll stay here if you want."

She shook her head. "The only thing you had that was of value to us is lost."

Jared felt relief and terror at the same time. He needed to see Arthur, but he had nothing else to offer. "We didn't have the Guide," he said. "We couldn't have given it to you then, but maybe we can get it back now."

The green-eyed elf turned back with a

scowl. "I have no further interest in your tales."

"I . . . I can prove it." Jared reached back into his hood, pulled out Thimbletack, and set him down in the grass. "I told you our house brownie had the book. This is Thimbletack."

The little brownie took off his hat and made a low bow, trembling slightly. "Great Lady, I know how this must look, but it is true I took the book."

"Your manners become you." She glanced at them both and then was silent for a moment.

Jared shifted impatiently as Thimbletack climbed up Jared's leg and slid back into his hiding place. The green-eyed elf's silence unnerved Jared, but he forced himself to stay quiet. This might be their last chance to convince her.

Finally she continued. "Our time to punish and to command is past. The moment we feared is upon us. Mulgarath has gathered a great army and is using the Guide to make it even more fearsome."

Jared nodded, although he was puzzled. He couldn't think of anything Mulgarath could do with the Guide that would make an army more dangerous. It was just a book.

"Promise me this, mortal child," the green-eyed elf said. "If Arthur's field guide comes again into your possession while you look for your mother, you will give it to us so

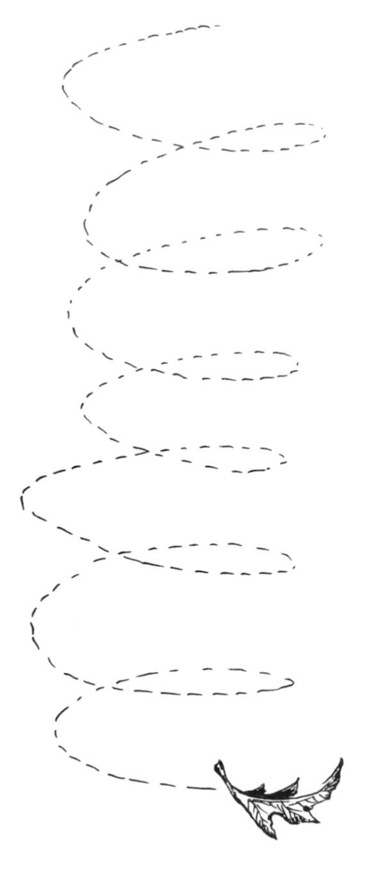

that it can be destroyed."

Jared nodded, giddily agreeing to anything that meant he would be able to see Arthur. "I will. I'll bring it—"

"No," she said. "When it is time, we will come to you." She pointed upward and spoke something in a strange language. A single leaf spiraled from a high branch of an old oak. It drifted slowly, as though it were falling through water instead of air. "Your audience with Arthur Spiderwick will last as long as it takes that leaf to fall to the ground."

Jared looked up toward where she pointed. As slowly as the leaf was moving, it still seemed too fast. "What if that isn't enough time?"

She smiled coldly. "Time is something that neither of us has the luxury of anymore, Jared Grace." But Jared barely noticed, because walking toward them from the trees was a man in a tweed coat, with graying patches of hair on the sides of his balding head. Leaves swept around him and dropped in a carpet in front of him so that his feet never touched the ground. He adjusted his spectacles nervously and peered at Jared.

Jared could not help grinning. Arthur Spiderwick looked just like the picture in the library. Now everything would be all right. His great-great-uncle would explain what to do, and that would be that.

"Uncle Arthur," Jared began. "I'm Jared."

A man in a tweed coat

"I do not believe I could possibly be your uncle, child," Arthur said stiffly. "To the best of my knowledge, my sister has no sons whatsoever."

"Well, actually, you're my great-great-uncle," Jared said, suddenly unsure of himself. "But that's not important."

"That's nonsense."

This wasn't going the way it was supposed to at all. "You've been gone a long time," Jared explained carefully.

Arthur scowled. "A few months, perhaps."

Thimbletack spoke up, climbing out of his hiding place and onto Jared's shoulder. "Listen to the boy—it is the only way. We cannot afford to delay."

Arthur peered down at the brownie and blinked twice. "Hello, old man! How I have missed you! Is my Lucy well? What about my wife? Will you give them a message for me?"

"Listen!" Jared interrupted. "Mulgarath has my mother, and you're the only one who knows what to do."

"Me?" Arthur asked. "Why should I know what to do?" He pushed his spectacles higher. "I would imagine that I would advise—wait, how old are you?"

"Nine," Jared replied, dreading what would come next.

"I would say that you should stay safe and leave the handling of such dangerous creatures to your elders."

"Didn't you hear me?" Jared shouted. "MULGARATH HAS MY MOTHER! THERE ARE NO ELDERS!"

"I understand," Arthur said. "However, you must—"

"No, you *don't* understand!" Jared couldn't

stop himself. It felt too good to finally just scream at someone. "You don't even know how long you've been here! Lucinda is older than you now! You don't know *anything.*"

Arthur opened his mouth as if to speak and then closed it. He looked pale and shaky, but Jared found it hard to care. His eyes burned with unshed tears. On the other side of the ring of mushrooms the single leaf was drifting ever closer to the ground.

"Mulgarath is a very dangerous ogre," Arthur said quietly. He didn't look at Jared when he spoke. "Even the elves do not know how to stop him."

"He has a dragon, too," Jared said.

Arthur looked up suddenly with interest. "A dragon? Really?" Then he shook his head and his shoulders slumped. "I can't tell you how to deal with any of this. I'm sorry—I simply don't know."

Jared wanted to plead, to demand, but no words came.

Arthur took a step closer, and when he

spoke, his voice was very gentle. "Child, if I always knew what to do, would I be here, trapped with the elves, never to see my own family again?"

"I guess not," Jared said, closing his eyes. The leaf had reached his height. It wouldn't be long now before his time was up.

"I can't give you a solution," Arthur said. "All I can give you is information. I wish I could do more."

He continued. "Goblins run in small packs, usually no more than ten. They follow Mulgarath because they're afraid of him—otherwise you would never see so many in one place. Without him leading them, they would fall into squabbling. But even with him, they probably aren't very organized.

"As for ogres, Mulgarath is typical of their kind. They're master shape-shifters—clever, sly, and cruel. Strong, too, unfortunately. One flaw that might help you is that they are often vain and prone to bragging."

"Like in the 'Puss in Boots' story?" Jared asked.

"Exactly." Arthur's eyes gleamed as he spoke. "Ogres think a lot of themselves and want you to think a lot of them as well. They love to hear themselves talk. And the normal protections—like that garment you're wearing—are next to useless. They're too powerful.

"As for dragons . . . well, I must confess everything I know about them was culled from other researchers."

"Other researchers? You mean there are other people researching faeries?"

Arthur nodded. "All over the world. Did you know there are faeries on every continent? There are variations, of course, much like with any other animal. But I digress.

"The subtype of dragon is probably of the European wyrm variety most common to this region. Very poisonous. I remember one account where a dragon lived on cow's milk—it got huge and its venom poisoned everything, scorched the grass, and made the water undrinkable."

"Wait!" Jared exclaimed. "Our water burns your mouth if you drink it—our well water."

"A very bad sign." Arthur sighed heavily and shook his head. "Dragons are quick, but they can be killed the same as any other creature. The difficulty, of course, is the poison. It

"A very bad sign."

grows stronger as the dragon grows, and only a very small number of creatures are fast enough and brave enough to go after a dragon, the way a mongoose attacks a cobra."

Jared looked at the leaf—it was almost to the ground. Arthur followed the look. "My time talking to you is almost done. Will you give Lucinda a message for me?"

"Sure. Of course." Jared nodded.

"Tell her—" But whatever Arthur was going to say was lost in the leaves that whorled around him, obscuring him from view. A tornado of leaves circled upward and then . . . nothing. Jared looked for the elf, but she was gone as well.

As Jared left the boundary of the grove, he saw Byron clawing in the dirt. Simon sat on the griffin's back, petting the creature to calm it. Behind him, Mallory held the dwarven sword

"It's your turn to trust us."

aloft, the metal gleaming in the sun. Hogsqueal sat at the beast's neck, looking positively miserable.

"What are you doing here?" Jared asked. "I thought you said you trusted me."

"And we do," said Mallory. "That's why we waited here instead of rushing in and hauling you out."

"We even have a plan." Simon held up a loop of rope. "Come on. You can tell us what you found out from the elves on the way."

"So, now," said Mallory, "it's your turn to trust us."

"I caught the humans."

Chapter Four

IN WHICH Everything Goes into the Fire

As he crossed the highway, Jared tried not to jostle the deliberately loose knots that kept his hands bound behind his back. He marched behind a similarly bound Mallory and avoided looking up at the distant shadow of Byron and Simon flying overhead—their only means of escape if things were to go wrong and the quickest way out if things were to go right.

Hogsqueal poked Jared with the tip of the dwarven sword. "Hurry up, nose pickers."

"Cut it out," Jared said, nearly stumbling.

Thimbletack squirmed against the back of his neck. "We're not even inside yet, and that thing is sharp," Jared said.

"Right," the hobgoblin snickered. "My bad, lump-meat."

"Leave Jared alone, or I'm going to *show* you how to use a sword," Mallory hissed, then suddenly went still.

The trees on that side of the highway were almost entirely leafless, blackened, and dead. The few remaining leaves hung from the branches like bats. The trees looked less real than the dwarves' ironwood trees. Just beyond, Jared could see the junkyard.

The gate was rusted open, and the worn dirt path was overgrown with patches of dead weeds. A NO TRESPASSING sign was stuck in the ground at an odd angle. Old cars, tires, and other trash were stacked in haphazard piles

that resembled swells of sand along a beach. And ahead Jared could see the palace clearly. Its spires gleamed with glass and tin in the full light of the sun.

Jared saw several goblins peering out of the rusted heap of a car. Two sniffed the air and a third began to bark. Then the goblins started to crawl from the vehicle. Each lifted a toadlike head and gnashed teeth of glass and bone. They carried dwarf-forged pikes and curved swords.

"You say you captured both?"

"Say something," Jared whispered to Hogsqueal.

"I caught the humans," Hogsqueal called. "No thanks to you trash hounds!"

A large goblin scuttled closer. His teeth were made of bottle glass, and they shimmered in the sunlight—brown, green, and clear. He was dressed in a ragged coat with tarnished buttons and a frayed tricornered hat. The hat in particular caught Jared's eye because it was dyed a strange ruddy brown. Flies buzzed close. "You say *you* captured both?"

"Easily, O large Wormrat," Hogsqueal bragged. "There they were, the girl swinging around this sword right here—sharp, isn't it?—but I was too fast for them! I . . ." Wormrat eyed him, and the hobgoblin's words trailed off. "Okay," he started again. "They were sleeping and I—"

The goblins began to bark loudly. Whether it was laughter or something else, Jared wasn't sure.

"I still caught the scallywags! They're *my* prisoners," Hogsqueal said, raising Mallory's sword. It looked huge in his small hands and was wobbling slightly.

Wormrat barked, and the tip of the sword drooped. Jared glanced upward to see if Simon and Byron were nearby, but they were either well hidden or gone. Jared hoped for what seemed like the millionth time that Simon would be able to control the griffin.

"We do what *I* say," said Wormrat. "Bring them!"

Mallory and Jared were pushed and pulled through the junkyard by a barking mass of goblins. They had to be careful not to step on the jagged pieces of metal that stuck up from the dry dirt at odd angles. Whenever Mallory and Jared slowed, the goblins shoved them and poked them with weapons. Rust from the cars streaked Jared's jeans as he squeezed through the narrow passageways between them. Finally they were led into a clearing where a dozen more goblins were lazing around a fire. Smallish bones were scattered among the debris.

Wormrat grunted and pointed toward a blue car close to the fire. "Tie the prisoners there."

"We should take them to the Palace of Trash," Hogsqueal said, but he sounded halfhearted.

"Quiet!" barked the big goblin. "*I* give commands."

A grinning goblin used a coil of rusty wire to attach Jared and Mallory's tether to the car. As the goblin wrapped the cord around the side mirror, Jared could smell his rotten breath and could see his strange, mottled skin, the hair tufting from his ears, the dead white of his eyes, and the long, quivering whiskers that stuck up from his face. The other goblins stood in a circle, leering and waiting.

"Back to your posts, lazy dogs!" bellowed the large goblin. Then, turning to the goblins that had already been there when he arrived, he scowled. "And the prisoners had better be where I leave them! I go report them to Mulgarath!" Barking, most of his goblins trickled back to their patrols as he left, but a few remained behind to sit around the fire.

Jared wriggled his hands. He was sure the knots were still loose enough for him to get free, but he was less sure they were going to be able to get past all of those goblins.

Jared and Mallory sat in the cold, sandy dirt for what felt like hours, watching the goblins pick up small lizards and toss them into the fire. The sky began to darken, the sun lighting slashes of gold across the waning day.

"Maybe this wasn't such a great plan after all," Mallory said softly. "We're nowhere near Mom, and I don't know where Simon is."

"But we're almost there," Jared whispered back. Their hands were close enough that he could take one of hers and squeeze it.

"What are they waiting for?" she asked with a groan.

"Maybe for the big one to come back," Jared replied.

Across the fire one of the goblins threw a wriggling black thing into the flames. "They never burn," the goblin said. "I wish they would burn."

"You still couldn't eat 'em," said another.

A soft voice from Jared's hood reminded him that Thimbletack was still with them. "Take a gander," whispered the brownie, "salamander."

Jared looked near his legs. One of the lizardlike things was next to his shoe. It was an opalescent black, with front legs and a long body that tapered to a tail. It was swallowing what appeared to be the tail of another.

"Jared," Mallory said. "Look in the fire. What are they?"

He leaned forward as far as his bonds would let him. There in the flames were all of the salamanders he'd seen the goblins toss. But instead of being scorched, they were sitting calmly as the blaze burned around them. As Jared stared, a few of the creatures moved slightly, one twisting its head and another scuttling deeper into the blaze. They really were immune to the fire.

He tried to think back to Arthur's Guide. He thought there was something on salamanders, but the images blurred in his mind. These little creatures looked like another illustration, but he couldn't quite put his finger on it. He was too nervous to concentrate—too full of thoughts of his mother and brother and of the goblins so close by.

A few moments later one of the goblins scurried over and poked Jared's stomach with a dirty claw. "They look so tasty. I could bite off one whole rosy cheek. I bet it would be sweet as candy." A long line of drool hit the dirt next to Jared.

Jared swallowed and looked over at Hogsqueal. The hobgoblin was using the dwarven sword to poke at the fire. He didn't look up, and that made Jared even more nervous.

Another goblin followed Jared's glance. "Wormrat will think he did it," the goblin said, pointing to Hogsqueal. "He was making a fuss before."

Hogsqueal stood up. "Of all the monkey-toasted, cracker-jack-headed . . ."

A third goblin approached, running its tongue over jagged teeth. "So much meat."

"Get away from him!" Mallory said. She pulled her hand out of Jared's. Only then did Jared realize he'd been clutching Mallory so tightly that his fingernails had dug into her skin.

"Would you rather we ate *you* instead?" asked the goblin sweetly. "Sugar and spice and everything nice. If that's what little girls are made of . . . sounds tasty to me!"

"Eat this!" Mallory said. She pulled her hands free and punched him in the face.

"The sword!" Jared yelled to Hogsqueal, trying to work his wrists out of the rope. The hobgoblin glanced at Jared once, then dropped the dwarven sword and ran from the clearing.

"Coward!" Jared yelled furiously. Free of his bindings, he ran toward the fire, but two goblins grabbed hold of his legs and toppled him into the dirt. Crawling forward until his hand could reach the blade, Jared swung the sword hilt-first to his sister. His hand stung, and he realized with dazed fascination that he had cut himself. More goblins jumped onto his back, pinning him in the dirt.

"Get away from him!" Mallory advanced, sword flashing as she swung it through the air. The goblins backed away from her. She whipped the blade at them. The goblins leaped off Jared and scrambled for their own weapons.

"Go! Run!" she yelled. A goblin jumped on her back, biting her shoulder.

Jared grabbed the goblin's arm and tugged it off his sister. Mallory kicked another that

"Get away from him!"

was approaching. One of the goblins picked up a dwarf-forged pike and swung it at Mallory. She parried it and then lunged, stabbing the goblin with her blade. As the creature howled, Mallory froze, realizing what she'd done. Blood stained the silver sword. The goblin fell, but others were rushing up fast and Mallory was still staring.

A screech above them broke her trance. Byron swooped toward the clearing and the goblins scattered, diving underneath trash for cover. The griffin's wings beat heavily, making the dirt dance.

"Come on," Jared said, grabbing at Mallory's arm. Together they leaped onto the rusted hood of a station wagon and then jumped down into a narrow path of corroded fencing. They ran past an overturned bathtub and a stack of tires. A series of doors were leaned up against a refrigerator, and as they passed them, Jared stopped abruptly. There, lying on a carpet of corrugated metal, was a cow.

It was a massive structure.

Chapter Five

IN WHICH They Find the Meaning of "Here There Be Dragons"

By reflex, Jared looked behind him, but the goblins were no longer there. The griffin landed with a clatter of claws on top of a car, denting it, and immediately began to groom himself like a cat. Simon grinned from Byron's back.

Jared turned to Mallory, but she was staring at the cow. It was chained to the ground, lowing softly, eyes wide enough to show the whites. Her udder was covered in what appeared to be writhing black snakes jostling for a position at her reddened teats. They blackened the metal sheeting on the ground beneath her like a squirming carpet. After a moment Jared realized the creatures were larger salamanders.

"What are those things doing?" Mallory asked. The bloodstained sword hung limply from her hand, and Jared was overwhelmed with the impulse to take it from her and clean it before she'd have a chance to notice.

He stepped closer to the cow instead. "Drinking the milk, I think."

"Ugh," Simon said, squinting down from Byron's back. "Weird."

Several more salamanders were lying in the dirt, their scales dull and their bodies wriggling. They were far larger than the tiny finger-length ones Jared and Mallory had seen in the fire.

"They're shedding their skin," Simon said. "What *are* they?"

Jared shook his head. "Fire-resistant salamanders. But they aren't supposed to get big like this. They look almost like . . ." But he wasn't quite sure what it was they reminded him of. Something nagged at the back of his mind.

At that moment Byron darted forward and seized one of the wriggling black creatures in his beak, tossed it into the air, and gulped it down. Then he seized another and another.

Greedily he went for an even larger one, as long as Jared's arm, curled up in the sun. It turned and hissed, and suddenly Jared knew what he was looking at.

"They're dragons," he said. "They're all dragons."

Out of the corner of his eye Jared saw something moving toward them, fast as a whip. He whirled, but the black thing hit him hard in the chest. Falling backward, he only had time to throw his hands up over his face before the thick body of a dragon as long as a couch scrabbled over him. Jared's head struck the ground, and for a moment everything went hazy.

"Jared!" Mallory howled. The dragon opened its mouth to show hundreds of teeth,

thin as needles. Jared froze. He was too terrified to move. His skin burned where the slick body had touched him.

Mallory chopped hard with her sword, catching the dragon's tail. Black blood spurted as the dragon turned toward her.

Jared got to his feet, dizzy and shivering. His skin was reddened, and the cut he'd gotten earlier throbbed angrily. "Watch out," he called. "It's poisonous!"

"Byron!" Simon yelled, pointing toward the black shape that was hurtling after Mallory. "Byron! Get it!"

The griffin swung up into the air with a screech. Jared looked after Byron and Simon desperately. How would Mallory escape the dragon now? She was cutting and thrusting as best as she could, but the dragon was too fast. Its body coiled and leaped like a snake, small forearms clutching and gripping, mouth so wide it seemed like it could swallow her whole. Mallory couldn't last. Jared had to do something.

Jared grabbed the nearest thing—a piece of metal—and hurled it at the dragon. The creature spun again and started toward him, lightning fast, jaws open. It hissed.

The griffin streaked down from the sky, talons reaching for the dragon, beak ripping at its back. The dragon coiled around Byron, wrapping its tail tight enough to choke. Simon hung on desperately as the griffin's wings

The dragon coiled around Byron.

pushed them back up into the air. The dragon twisted, teeth sinking into Byron's feathered and furred body. Then the griffin's wings missed a beat, and in the sudden drop, Simon slipped off.

Jared ran toward his twin as he plummeted toward the junkyard. Simon fell onto a pile of screen windows and his left arm twisted at an odd angle.

"Simon?" Jared knelt down beside him.

Simon moaned softly and used his other arm to push himself into a sitting position. His left cheek and neck were red from dragon poison, but the rest of his skin looked far too pale.

"Are you okay?" Jared whispered. Mallory touched Simon's arm gingerly.

Simon winced and stood up shakily. Above them the dragon and griffin were locked together, a writhing, looping knot of scales and skin. The dragon's teeth were embedded deep in Byron's neck, and the griffin was flying erratically.

"He's going to die." Simon limped toward the cow with her mass of dragon fingerlings.

"What are you doing?" Jared called after him.

When Simon turned back to them, tears were running down his face. As Jared watched him, Simon—who had never killed anything, who always carried spiders outside—stepped on the head of one of the baby dragons, crushing it into a smear under his shoe. It squealed. Dragon blood stained the ground and melted the edge of Simon's heel.

"Look!" he screamed. "Look what I'm doing to your babies!

The dragon turned in midair, and Byron seized the opportunity. Plunging his beak into

the creature's neck, he rent it wide. The dragon went limp in Byron's claws.

"Simon! You did it!" Mallory said.

Simon watched Byron land near them. His feathers were smeared with blood, and he shook himself. Then, dropping the body of the large dragon, Byron resumed eating the babies.

"This isn't going the way we planned," Simon said.

"But we're closer to the palace now," Jared said. "Mom has to be there."

"Do you think you can make it, Simon?" Mallory asked, although she didn't look very well herself, with her cheek cut and her jacket slashed at the shoulder.

Simon nodded, his face grim. "I can, but I don't know about Byron."

"We have to leave him here," Jared said. "I

think he'll be okay. The poison doesn't seem to affect him."

Byron gulped down another squirming black salamander and regarded the Grace kids with his strange golden eyes. Simon petted him carefully on the nose. "Yeah, he seems to like these dragons more than anything I used to feed him."

"Let me see if I can do something about your arm," Mallory said. "I think it's broken." She used her undershirt to tie Simon's arm neatly against his side.

"Are you sure you know what you're doing?" Simon asked, wincing.

"Sure I'm sure," Mallory said, tying the white fabric tight.

They marched in the direction of the palace. It was a massive structure made of what looked like cement or stucco, mixed with gravel, glass, and aluminum cans. It looked less molded than poured and in some places resembled dried lava. The windows were strangely shaped, as though the creator had fitted the house around whatever refuse he had found. Lights flickered inside. Several spires came to delicate points off the main roof, which was black with tar and covered in overlapping layers of glass and tin that looked like fish scales. As Jared got closer, he noticed that the main gate was made of old brass headboards. Beyond the gate was a deep trench dug in the earth, studded with jagged, rusty metal and chunks of broken glass. The drawbridge was down.

"Shouldn't there be goblins guarding it or something?" Mallory asked.

The drawbridge was down.

Jared looked around. In the distance he could see tendrils of smoke coming from what he guessed were goblin camps.

"It's going to be dark soon," Simon said.

"It just seems too easy," Jared said. "Like a trap."

"Trap or not, we're going to have to keep going," Mallory said.

Simon nodded. Jared still thought that Simon looked a little too pale and wondered how much pain he was in. At least the red skin had faded somewhat.

Stepping onto the drawbridge cautiously, Jared braced himself for something to happen. He kept glancing at the jagged glass jutting up out of the moat. Then he raced across. Mallory and Simon paused a moment, then ran after him.

As they entered the palace, they found

themselves in a large hall constructed from salvaged materials and what seemed to be cement. The archways were trimmed with bent chrome fenders. Hubcaps hung from the ceiling on rusted chains, flickering with the uncertain light of dozens of yellowed candles and dripping with wax. Set inside one wall was a fireplace large enough to roast Jared in.

It was eerily quiet. Their footsteps echoed in the dim rooms, and their shadows loomed along the walls.

They walked farther, passing musty-smelling couches covered in threadbare throws.

"Do we have anything even remotely resembling a plan?" Mallory asked.

"Nope," Jared said.

"No," Simon echoed.

"Hush," said Thimbletack. "Have a care. I hear something over there."

They paused a moment, listening. There was a faint noise that sounded almost like music.

"I think it's coming from here," Jared said, pushing open a door that had been decorated with more than a dozen knobs. Inside the room was a tall, long table made from a plank of wood on top of three sawhorses. Thick candles that smelled of burning hair covered most of the table. Rivulets of melted wax ran down the sides. Also set on the table were platters of food—long, greasy trays of roasted frogs, half-eaten apples, the tail and bones of a large fish. Flies buzzed greedily around the remains. From somewhere in the room came a series of high-pitched notes.

"What is that?" Simon asked, squeezing past a single large chair. Then he stopped, looking at something Jared and Mallory couldn't see. They scrambled over to him.

A large urn sat on the floor underneath an open window. There, in the wavering light, Jared could see sprites trapped in honey, sinking as though it were quicksand. The sprites' tiny cries were the sound he had heard before.

Simon reached in to pull the sprites free, but the honey was heavy and clung to their thin wings, tearing them. The sprites squealed as he set each one down on the table in a sticky, sodden heap. One was completely still and lay there limply, like a doll. Jared looked away, staring out the window.

"Do you think there are more in there?" Mallory whispered.

"I think so," Simon said. "At the bottom."

"We have to keep going." Jared moved toward another doorway. The thought of the tiny drowned faeries made him feel queasy.

"The palace is just too quiet," said Mallory as she followed him.

"Mulgarath can't be here all the time," Jared said. "Maybe we got lucky. Maybe we can just find Mom and get out."

Mallory nodded, but she didn't look convinced.

They passed by a map hung on a wall. It looked much like Arthur's old map, but the places had been renamed. Jared noticed that over the junkyard had been written MULGARATH'S PALACE and that lettered across the entire top of the paper was MULGARATH'S DOMAIN.

"Look!" Simon said. Ahead of them was a large room with a throne at its center. Surrounding the throne were overlapping carpets in different patterns, all of them moth-eaten and worn. The throne was made of metal, welded together and jagged in places.

At one end of the room was a spiral staircase, each step a plank suspended on two long metal chains. The whole thing looked like a web, wobbling slightly with each breeze. In the dim light the stairs looked impossible to climb.

Mallory pulled herself onto the first rung. It swung alarmingly. She tried to step onto the next one, but her legs were too short.

"These steps are too far apart!" she exclaimed.

"Perfect for an ogre," Simon pointed out.

She finally managed to catch the second step, flop onto it chest-first, and pull herself up that way.

The stairs looked impossible to climb.

"Simon's not going to be able to climb this," she said.

"I can . . . I'll be okay," Simon insisted, lifting himself awkwardly onto the first step.

Mallory shook her head. "You're going to fall."

"Hold on tight," Thimbletack called from Jared's hood. "You'll be all right." Then Jared watched in amazement as each step swung closer and held steady for his siblings to climb onto it. With one working arm and Mallory's help, Simon climbed up the stairs.

"It would behoove you to move," said Thimbletack.

"Oh, right." Jared worked his way up the steps. Even with the brownie's help, his heart thundered as he went higher and higher. The cut on his hand burned where he gripped the chains. Glancing down into the darkness below made Jared momentarily dizzy.

At the top they found themselves in a hallway with three doors, all mismatched.

"Let's try the middle one," Simon said.

"We made so much noise just now," said Mallory. "Where is everyone? It's eerie."

"We have to keep going," Jared said, repeating his words from earlier.

Mallory sighed and opened the door. It opened onto a large room with a balcony made of mismatched stones and chains. Giant cathedral windows, filled with translucent mosaics made of glass shards, covered the other wall. Their mother was in one corner, bound, gagged, and unconscious. In the other corner, hanging from ropes and a pulley, was their dad.

"What are you doing here?"

Chapter Six

IN WHICH All Hell Breaks Loose

"What are you doing here?" Jared asked. Behind him he heard Simon and Mallory exclaim "Dad!" together. Their father's black hair looked slightly mussed and his shirt was untucked on one side, but it was definitely him.

Their father's eyes went wide. "Jared! Simon! Mallory! Thank goodness you're okay."

Jared furrowed his brow. Something about this didn't feel right. He looked around the room again. Out beyond the balcony he saw goblins milling in the gloom, holding torches. What was going on?

"Quick," Mallory said. "We have to move. Jared, untie Mom. I'll work on Dad."

Jared leaned down and touched his mother's pale cheek. It felt cold and clammy. Her glasses were gone. "Mom's unconscious," he said.

"Is she breathing?" Mallory asked, halting.

Jared put his hand against his mother's lips and felt the ghost of her breath. "She's okay. She's alive."

"Did you see Mulgarath?" Simon asked his father. "The ogre?"

"There was some commotion outside," Mr. Grace said. "I didn't see anything after that."

Mallory fumbled with the pulley and managed to lower her dad's hands. "How did they get you all the way from California?"

Their dad shook his head wearily. "Your mother called to say how worried she was—all three of you acting strange and then going missing. I came as soon as I could, but the monsters were already at the house. It was terrible. At first I couldn't believe what was happening. And they kept talking about a book. What is this book?"

"Our uncle Arthur—" Jared began.

"More like Mom's great-uncle, our great-great-uncle," Mallory said as she picked at the knots.

"Right. Well, he was interested in faeries." Jared untied his mother as he talked, but even free from her bonds, she didn't move. Jared smoothed back her hair, wishing she would open her eyes.

"His brother got eaten by a troll," Simon put in.

Jared nodded, looking nervously around. How long before they were discovered? Did they really have time for this? Now that they had found their mother, they had to get out as quickly as possible. "And so he made this book that was all about faeries. It had stuff in it that even some of the faeries themselves didn't know."

"Because they mostly don't bother with one another, it seems," Mallory said.

How were they going to get their mother down the stairs? Could their dad carry her? Jared tried to concentrate on explaining. They had to make sure their dad would understand. "But the faeries didn't want one guy to have that much power over them, so they tried to get the book back. When he wouldn't give it to them, they took him instead."

"The elves did," Simon said.

"Really?" said their father with a strange gleam in his eye.

Jared sighed. "Look, I know it sounds unbelievable, Dad, but look around. Does this look like the set of one of your movies?"

"I believe you," their father said softly.

"To make a very long story short," Mallory said, "we found the book."

"Except we lost the book again," said Simon. "The ogre has it."

"And he's got a really idiotic plan to take over the world," Mallory put in.

Their father's eyebrows rose, but he only

said, "So, now that the book is gone, all of the knowledge is gone with it. There's no other copy? That seems like a shame."

"Jared remembers a lot," Simon said. "I bet he could make a book of his own."

Mallory nodded. "And we learned some stuff along the way—right, Jared?"

Jared smiled, looking down. "I guess so," he said finally. "But I wish I remembered more."

Their father flexed his newly freed wrists and stretched his legs. "I'm sorry that I wasn't here sooner. I shouldn't have left you kids and your mom alone. And I want to make it up to you. I want to stay."

"We missed you too, Dad," Simon said.

Mallory looked down at her boots. "Yeah."

Jared said nothing. Something about this was too easy. It just felt wrong. "Mom?" he said softly, and shook her.

Dad spread his arms wide. "Come and give your father a hug."

Simon and Mallory embraced him. Jared looked down at his mother and reluctantly started to cross the room, when his dad said, "I want us all to be together from now on."

Jared froze. He wanted it so much to be true, but it didn't feel true. "Dad would never say that," he said.

His father grabbed hold of his arm. "Don't you *want* us to be a family again?"

"Of course I do!" Jared yelled, jerking his arm free and stepping back. "I want Dad to be less of a jerk, and for Mom to not be sad. I want my dad to stop talking about himself and his movies and his life all the time and remember that I'm the loser who almost got kicked out of school and Simon is the one who likes animals and Mallory is the fencer. But that's not going to happen and *you're not him.*"

As Jared looked up into the familiar hazel eyes of his father, they started to turn pale yellow. His father's body elongated, filling out, becoming a mammoth shape clad in the tattered remains of ancient finery. His hands became claws, and his dark hair twined together into branches. "Mulgarath," Jared said.

The ogre wrapped one arm around Mallory's neck and with the other arm grabbed Simon.

"Come here, Jared Grace!" Mulgarath's voice boomed, far deeper than their father's. He strode toward the balcony, still holding Simon and Mallory. "Give yourself up. Otherwise, I will heave your brother and sister into my moat of glass and iron."

"Leave them alone," Jared said shakily. "You have the book."

"You're not him".

"I can't do that," Mulgarath said. "You know the secret that speeds the growth of dragons and how to kill them. You know the weaknesses of my goblins. I cannot allow you to make another Guide."

"Run!" Mallory yelled. "Get Mom and run!" She bit the ogre.

He laughed and pressed his arm tighter against her, heaving her up into the air. "Do you think your feeble strength is enough to match mine, human girl?"

Simon kicked, but the hulking monster didn't seem to notice.

A groan came from the other end of the room, and Jared half turned. His mother stirred and opened her eyes. They went wide. "Richard? I thought I heard . . . oh my God!"

"Everything's going to be okay, Mom," Jared said, wishing for his voice to stay even. Somehow her seeing all of this made it more horrible.

"Mom, tell him to run!" Mallory shouted. "Both of you! Go!"

"Quiet, girl, or I'll break your neck." The ogre growled, but when he addressed Jared, his voice became soothing. "It's a fair trade, isn't it? Your life for the lives of your brother and sister and mother?"

"Jared, what's happening?" their mother called.

Jared tried to stay calm. He was afraid to die, but it would be so much worse to watch his brother, sister, and mother get hurt. Already the ogre's fingers seemed to be loosening, ready to drop Simon and Mallory at any moment. "You won't free us—even if I promise not to make another Guide!"

Mulgarath shook his head slowly, eyes full of dark satisfaction.

"Put them down!" Their mother's voice was panicked. "Put my children down! Jared, what are you doing?"

It was then that Jared noticed Mallory's sword lying on the floor.

Seeing the sword made Jared focus. He had to concentrate—to come up with a plan. Jared remembered what Arthur had said about ogres—they liked to brag. He only hoped that this one would. "I'll give up and come over there."

"No, you idiot!" Mallory shouted.

"Jared, don't!" Simon yelled.

"But before I do . . ." Jared swallowed hard and hoped that the ogre would take the bait. "There's something I want to know. Why are you doing all of this? Why now?"

Mulgarath smiled toothily. "You humans take everything and keep the best part for

"Why are you doing all of this?"

yourselves. You live in palaces, dine on banquets, and clothe yourselves in fine silks and velvets like royalty. We, who live forever, who have magic, who have *power,* are supposed to lie down and let your kind trample us into the ground. No more.

"I have been planning this for a long time. First I thought I would have to wait for my dragons to mature. I have time on my side. But with the Guide I was able to step up my plans. As long as they have enough milk, the dragons are quite docile, you know. And I am sure by now you've realized how fast the milk makes them grow and how powerful they become.

"The elves are too feeble to stop me, and the humans will never see it coming. It is my time—the time of Mulgarath! The time of goblins! The land will have a new master!"

Jared tipped his head to the side, hoping Mulgarath was too busy talking to notice, and whispered into his hood. "Thimbletack, can you make the chains on the railing attach to Mallory's and Simon's legs?"

Thimbletack wriggled and whispered back. "I'd have to get to the ground without making a sound."

"I'll keep him talking," Jared whispered, then raised his voice, addressing the ogre. "So why did you have to kill the dwarves? I don't understand. They wanted to help you."

"They had their own little dream of a world built of iron and gold. But what fun would it be to rule a world like that? No, I want a world of flesh and blood and bone." The ogre smiled again, as though pleased with the way that had sounded, then looked down at Jared. "Enough talk. Come here."

"What about the Guide?" Jared asked. "At least tell me where that is."

"I think not," Mulgarath said. "It is beyond you now."

"I just want to know if I could have found it," Jared said.

A cruel smile twisted the ogre's features. "Indeed, had you been more clever, you could have found it. A pity that you are a mere human child, no match for me at all. The book was beneath my throne this whole time."

"You know," Jared said, "we killed your dragons. I hope that doesn't put too much of a dent in your clever plan."

Mulgarath looked genuinely surprised. Then his brow knotted with anger.

Out of the corner of his eye Jared could see the chains unlinking and snaking across the floor like vipers. One wrapped around

Mallory's leg, and the other circled Simon's waist. When the metal touched her skin, Mallory flinched. A third chain crept toward Mulgarath's ankle, and Jared hoped that the ogre would not notice.

But Jared's pause was enough to catch Mulgarath's attention. He looked down and spotted Thimbletack skittering along the floor. The ogre kicked the brownie, his giant foot tossing Thimbletack across the room, where Thimbletack landed like a crumpled glove beside Mrs. Grace. The chains stopped moving. "What is this?" Mulgarath bellowed, stamping down on the links near his foot. "You sought to trick me?"

Jared ran forward and grabbed Mallory's silver sword.

Mulgarath laughed and dropped Simon and Mallory off the side of the balcony. They both screamed and then were silent, while their mother's scream went on and on. Jared didn't know if the chains had held. He didn't know anything.

Jared thought he might be sick. Rage filled him. Everything looked small and far away. He felt the weight of the sword in his hand as though it were the only real thing in the world. He raised it high. Someone far away was calling his name, but he didn't care. Nothing mattered anymore.

Then just as he was about to swing, he saw the look of satisfaction on the ogre's face—as if Jared were doing just what Mulgarath had expected . . . as if Jared were playing right into his hands. If he swung the sword, he would be matching his strength against the ogre's, and the ogre would win.

Abruptly Jared changed the direction of his blow and brought the point of the sword down hard, stabbing Mulgarath in the foot.

The ogre howled with surprise and pain, lifting his wounded foot. Jared dropped the sword and grabbed the chain that ran beneath the ogre's other foot, pulling with his full weight. Mulgarath stumbled backward, trying to regain his balance. But just as his calves hit the chain fence, Jared slammed into him again. The ogre's weight pulled the chains loose from the wall, and he went hurtling over the side.

Jared rushed to the edge of the balcony. To his immense relief, Simon and Mallory were dangling over the pit, chains wrapped around Simon's waist and Mallory's leg. They called up to him weakly.

Jared started to smile, but as he did, he saw Mulgarath, his fist clutching another chain, his body shifting into the shape of a squirming dragon. He began to writhe his way back up to them.

"Watch out!" Jared shouted.

Simon, hanging closer to the monster, tried to kick at it. He only made the chains swing dangerously.

Mallory and Simon screamed as Jared leaned out as far as he could and swung the sword again. This time it hit the ogre's chain, cutting through it and biting into the wall of the palace. Mulgarath started to transform once more. As the ogre fell toward the pit of jagged glass, his body became smaller and smaller until he finally became a swallow. The bird veered out of the pit, heading toward the assembled throng of goblins. In mere moments Mulgarath would lead that army into the palace. There would be no escape for the Grace family.

But then, as the bird turned, angling to fly back toward where the children stood, a hob-goblin's hand suddenly shot out and grabbed the bird out of the air. It happened so fast that Jared didn't have time to be surprised and the ogre didn't have time to shift again.

Hogsqueal bit off the bird's head and chewed twice with apparent enjoyment. "Cruddy mouth-breather," he said as he gulped it down.

Jared couldn't help it. He started to laugh.

"All this time and I never knew."

Epilogue

IN WHICH the Story of the Grace Children Comes to Its Conclusion

Jared sat down on the gleaming floor of Arthur's newly cleaned library and leaned against Aunt Lucinda's leg. Mallory knelt next to him, making stacks of old letters written in languages that none of them spoke. Simon flipped through an old book of sepia photographs while their mother poured hot tea into mugs.

All of that might have seemed normal if Hogsqueal wasn't seated on a nearby footstool, playing checkers with a bandaged and annoyed-looking Thimbletack.

Lucinda held up one of the paintings of the little girl from Arthur's desk. "I can't believe it. All this time and I never knew."

It had been three weeks since they had defeated Mulgarath, and Jared was finally starting to think things were going to *stay* okay. The goblins had dispersed into bickering groups. Byron was gone by the time they had left the palace, and he appeared to have eaten every last dragonet. Jared, Simon, Mallory, and their mother had all walked home from the dump. It had been a long walk, and they had been so tired that once they'd arrived home, they had collapsed into the piles of feathers and cloth that had been their beds without complaint or comment. It was dark when Jared had finally woken and noticed Thimbletack curled up on a pillow beside him, with Simon's tiny, marmalade cat nestled against the little brownie. Jared had smiled, taken a deep breath, and choked on the feathers.

Downstairs he'd found his mother cleaning up the kitchen. When Jared had walked into the room, she had hugged him tightly.

"I'm so sorry," she'd said.

Even though it had kind of made him feel like a baby, he'd hugged her back for a long time.

Later that week their mother had arranged for Lucinda to leave the asylum and come stay with them. Jared had been amazed to find his great-aunt, with a haircut and a new suit, sitting in the parlor one day after school. When Mulgarath died, his magic must have died with him, and although Lucinda often walked with a cane now, her back was as straight as it had ever been.

Mrs. Grace had been less miraculous in curing Jared's school troubles; he had been expelled. His mother had enrolled him and Simon in a private school nearby. She claimed the school had excellent art and science programs. Mallory decided to stay at the old school. She only had one year till she was in high school anyway and plenty still to prove to the J. Waterhouse fencing team.

For his part, Jared had locked Arthur's field guide in its metal trunk again. But after all that he still didn't know what to think. Were there creatures still after them? Had the ogre been the worst—or just the worst yet?

A breeze blew through the office, scattering papers and snapping Jared out of his thoughts. Simon jumped up, trying to catch hold of the letters.

"Did you leave a window open?" their mother asked Aunt Lucinda.

"I don't recall doing so," their great-aunt replied.

"I'll get it," Mallory said, and started toward the window.

Then a single leaf blew inside. It danced in the air, swooping and swirling, until it fell directly in front of Jared. The leaf was greenish brown, and Jared thought it might be from a maple tree. Written on the leaf in a delicate hand was Jared's name. He turned it over and read:

"It doesn't say where," Mallory said, reading over his shoulder.

"The grove, I guess," Jared said.

"You're not going to go, are you?" Simon asked.

"I'm going," said Jared. "I promised. I need to give them Arthur's field guide. I don't want anything like this to happen again."

"Then we're going with you," said Simon.

"I'm coming too," their mother said.

The three children looked at her with surprise, then glanced at each other.

"Don't forget me, dizzinits," Hogsqueal said.

"Don't forget *us,*" Thimbletack corrected.

Aunt Lucy reached for her cane. "I hope it isn't much of a walk?"

That night they left the house carrying lanterns, flashlights, and the field guide. It was weird to go looking for faeries with their mother in tow and Simon helping Aunt Lucy along. Up the hill they went, and then they carefully made their way down the other side.

Jared thought he heard a whisper of "Clever is as clever does," but it might have been only his memory or the wind.

The grove was lit with dozens upon dozens of sprites, whirring through the air, twinkling like giant fireflies, alighting on tree branches and settling in the grass. Elves sat on the ground—many more than the three the children had seen on their first visit—all clad in the deep colors of autumn as though to camouflage themselves with the forest.

The elves went quiet as the small group of humans made their way to the center of the clearing. There, standing among all of those seated, was the green-eyed elf, her expression unreadable. Beside her stood the leaf-horned elf, looking stern, and red-haired Lorengorm, who was smiling.

Thinking of Thimbletack, Jared made an awkward bow. The others followed his example.

"We brought the book," Jared said, and held it out to the green-eyed elf.

She smiled. "That is well. We must abide by our promises, and had you not, Simon would have had to stay with us for a very long time."

Simon shivered and stepped closer to Mallory. Jared scowled.

"But since you have done so," she continued, "we wish to return it to you for safekeeping."

"What?" Mallory said. Jared was astonished.

"You have proven that humans may use the

knowledge it contains for good. Therefore we return the Guide to you."

Lorengorm stepped forward. "We also wish to give you some measure of our gratitude for restoring peace to these lands. To that end we offer you a boon."

"A boon?" Hogsqueal puffed out his chest. "What do I get? How come these ninnyhammers get a reward when I'm the one that defeated Mulgarath?"

Several of the elves began to laugh, and Thimbletack gave Hogsqueal a stern look.

"Figures he wasn't coming along to be supportive," Mallory said.

"So what would you like, little hobgoblin?" asked the green-eyed elf.

"Well," Hogsqueal said, putting a finger to his mouth as if considering. "I'd like some kind of medal, definitely. Gold, with 'fearsome killer of ogres' on it. No, wait, how about 'supreme slayer of monsters'? Or—"

"Is that all?" asked Lorengorm.

"It should say 'supreme beetlehead,'" Simon whispered to Jared.

"I don't think so," said the hobgoblin. "I want a victory feast in my honor. And it should have quail's eggs—I love those—and pigeon baked in a pie shell and barbequed ca—"

"We'll consider your requests," the green-eyed elf said, barely hiding a smile behind her delicate hand. "But now I must ask the children to name the desire of their heart."

Jared looked at his brother and sister. At first they seemed thoughtful, and then smiles started to grow on their faces. Jared glanced back at his mother, who still seemed a bit confused, and his great-aunt, her face full of hope.

"We would like our great-great-uncle, Arthur Spiderwick, to have a choice whether to stay in Faerie or not."

"You understand," Lorengorm said, "that if he chooses to return to the mortal world, the

Watercolor study of Arthur and Lucinda Spiderwick, found in Arthur's study.

first time his foot touches the earth, he will become dust and ash."

Jared nodded. "I understand."

"We have anticipated your request," said the green eyed elf. With a wave of her hand the trees parted, and Byron stepped through. On his back was Arthur Spiderwick.

Jared heard the others gasp behind him. Arthur smiled at Jared briefly, and this time Jared noticed that his eyes were like Lucinda's, both sharp and kind. Arthur sat on the griffin awkwardly and petted him with a kind of awe. Then he looked over at Mallory and Simon. He adjusted his glasses.

"You are my great-great-niece and nephew, aren't you?" he said softly. "Jared didn't mention that he had a brother and a sister."

Jared nodded. He wondered if there was any way he could apologize for the things he

"This is fine work."

had said earlier. He wondered what Arthur thought of him.

"I'm Simon," said Simon. "This is Mallory, and this is our mom." Simon looked at Lucinda and hesitated.

"I'm glad to meet you," said Arthur. "You three children clearly have my inquisitive blood running through your veins. You might have had cause to regret it." He shook his head wryly. "It seems to have gotten you into a lot of scrapes. Luckily you three seem far more adept at getting yourselves out of trouble than I ever was." He smiled again, and this time his smile wasn't the least bit tentative. It was a wide grin that made him look very unlike the man in the painting.

"We're glad to see you too," Jared said. "We want to give your book back to you."

"My field guide!" Arthur said. He took it from Jared's hands and started flipping through it. "Look at this—who did these sketches?"

"I did," Jared said, his voice as soft as a whisper. "I know they aren't very good."

"Nonsense!" Arthur said. "This is fine work. I predict that you are going to be a great artist someday."

"Really?" Jared said.

Arthur nodded. "Really."

Thimbletack walked up to Arthur's shoes. "Good to see you, my old friend, but there are some things to mend. Here is Lucinda, who you know. She is not as she was long ago."

Arthur's breath caught as he finally recognized her. *She must look so old to him,* Jared thought. He tried to picture his mother as a young woman, looking at an elderly version of him, but it was too hard, too sad.

Lucinda smiled, and tears ran down her

cheeks. "Daddy!" she said. "You look just the way you did the day you left."

Arthur made a move to dismount.

"No!" Lucinda said. "You'll turn to dust." Leaning on her cane, she walked closer to where he stood.

"I'm sorry for all of the sadness I caused you and your mother," he said. "I'm sorry I tried to trick the elves. I should have never taken the risk. I've always loved you, Lucy. I always wanted to come home."

"You are home now," said Lucinda.

Arthur shook his head. "Elven magic has kept me alive too long. I have lived past the span of my years. It is my time to go, but seeing you, Lucy—I can go without sorrow."

"I just got you back," she said. "You can't die now."

Arthur bent down and spoke to her—soft

words that Jared could not hear—before he stepped off the griffin and into her embrace. As Arthur's foot touched the ground, his body turned to dust and then smoke. It swirled around Jared's great-aunt and then whirled up into the night sky and was gone.

Jared turned to Lucinda, expecting to see her crying, but her eyes were dry. She stared up at the stars and smiled. Jared slid his hand into hers.

"It's time for us to go home," Aunt Lucinda said. Jared nodded. He thought about everything that had happened, all of the things that he had seen, and suddenly realized how much he still had to sketch. After all, he was only at the beginning.

Here ends the tale of
THE GRACE CHILDREN

About TONY DiTERLIZZI . . .

A *New York Times* best-selling author, Tony DiTerlizzi created the Zena Sutherland Award–winning *Ted, Jimmy Zangwow's Out-of-This-World Moon Pie Adventure,* as well as illustrations in Tony Johnston's Alien and Possum beginning-reader series. Most recently, his brilliantly cinematic version of Mary Howitt's classic *The Spider and the Fly* was awarded a Caldecott Honor. In addition, Tony's art has graced the work of such well-known fantasy names as J.R.R. Tolkien, Anne McCaffrey, Peter S. Beagle, and Greg Bear as well as Wizards of the Coast's *Magic The Gathering*. He and his wife, Angela, reside with their pug, Goblin, in Amherst, Massachusetts. Visit Tony on the World Wide Web at www.diterlizzi.com.

and HOLLY BLACK

An avid collector of rare folklore volumes, Holly Black spent her early years in a decaying Victorian mansion where her mother fed her a steady diet of ghost stories and books about faeries. Accordingly, her first novel, *Tithe: A Modern Faerie Tale,* is a gothic and artful glimpse at the world of Faerie. Published in the fall of 2002, it received two starred reviews and a Best Book for Young Adults citation from the American Library Association. She lives in West Long Branch, New Jersey, with her husband, Theo, and a remarkable menagerie. Visit Holly on the World Wide Web at www.blackholly.com.

Tony and Holly continue to work day and night fending off angry faeries and goblins in order to bring the Grace children's story to you.

Through field, cave, and forest
this yarn has unspun
with our heroes victorious
and evil undone!

Yet all is not merry
as we reach this end
and must bid farewell
to a father, guide, . . . friend.

Though Arthur is taken,
what's given is vast!
His beloved Lucinda
is safe home at last.

Hogsqueal has eaten.
The Graces can rest.
And Thimbletack's back to
what brownies do best.

With everyone happy
and no longer vexed,
one question needs answering. . . .
What happens next?

Are there more ogres
and dragons to slay?
Is there more mayhem,
perhaps, on the way?

Ask Tony and Holly.
They'll swear that it's true.
But you still won't believe
what's coming for you!

For the time is upon us.
The Guide is at hand.
Soon Spiderwick's opus
will be read through the land.

So keep your eyes open.
And when you see it, do choose it!
Because knowledge is good. . . .
Just beware how you use it.

ACKNOWLEDGMENTS

Tony and Holly would like to thank
Steve and Dianna for their insight,
Starr for her honesty,
Myles and Liza for sharing the journey,
Ellen and Julie for helping make this our reality,
Kevin for his tireless enthusiasm and faith in us,
and especially Angela and Theo—
there are not enough superlatives
to describe your patience
in enduring endless nights
of Spiderwick discussion.

The text type for this book is set in Cochin.
The display types are set in Nevins Hand and Rackham.
The illustrations are rendered in pen and ink.
Production editor: Dorothy Gribbin
Art director: Dan Potash
Production manager: Chava Wolin